POWER, WISDOM, AND COURAGE

An Inktober Sketchbook

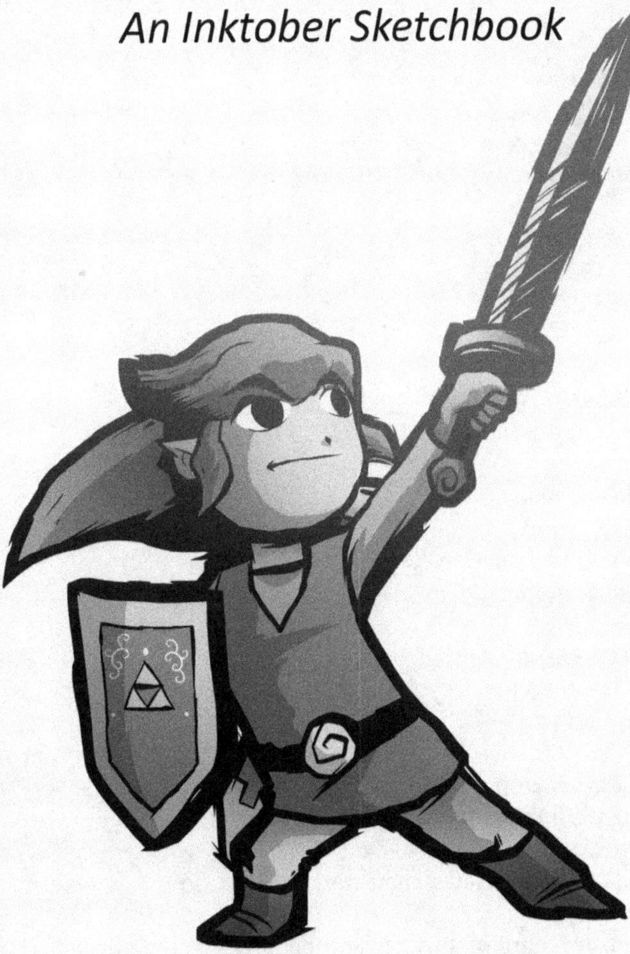

JAMES ART VILLE

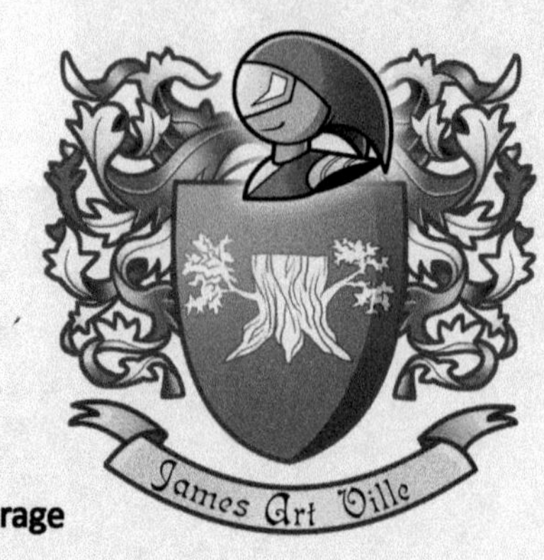

Power, Wisdom, and Courage
An Inktober Sketchbook

Copyright © 2024 by James Art Ville

Published by His Own Comics
Grants Pass, OR 97526
https://www.jamesartville.com
james@hallowstatum.com

ISBN Print: 978-1-951907-04-4
ISBN PDF: 978-1-951907-05-1
ISBN Mobi: 978-1-951907-06-8
ISBN ePub: 978-1-951907-07-5

First Printing - October 2024
Library of Congress Control Number: 2020916539

Edited by Ellie Ville and Alan Corona

Hylia Serif Beta font © Jack Sullivan
Hylian Symbols font © mdta

Inktober © 2009 Jake Parker
Linktober © 2015 Joel Siegel

J.P. Creative, LLC ("J.P. Creative") is a United States limited liability company with full ownership of the INKTOBER brands including, but not limited to, U.S. Reg. No. 5573543 and EUTM Reg. No. 017894645, associated stylizations, logos, etc.

The Legend of Zelda™ and all related characters © Nintendo

ILLUSTRATIONS BY JAMES ART VILLE

In 2009, Jake Parker challenged himself to make an illustration for every day during the month of October, a total of 31 drawings. Since then, he has encouraged artists all around the world to join him in this annual event where creators push themselves, hone their skill, and share their art with the world! As a fellow participant, I can testify to the positive impact this has had in my life as an artist.

The official Inktober website publishes a calendar of prompts to give artists a theme for each day. By no means is this binding as any artist who participates in Inktober can freely illustrate whatever they please. For 2019's Inktober, I decided to pass on the official calendar and opted in for a different one with a unique twist.

The Inktober movement was such a success that it sprung many variations, including one that struck a personal chord with me, Linktober. Named after the protagonist of the popular video game series, Link, this calendar is entirely dedicated to the creation of fan art for Nintendo's *The Legend of Zelda*.

As an avid gamer myself, I was thrilled at the opportunity to spend an entire month drawing some of my favorite fictional characters of all time. Inktober can be challenging for many artists if they don't feel the motivation to draw, especially if some of the prompts don't quite ignite creativity. By participating in Linktober, I was never short on passion every time I put pen to paper... er, I mean stylus to screen.

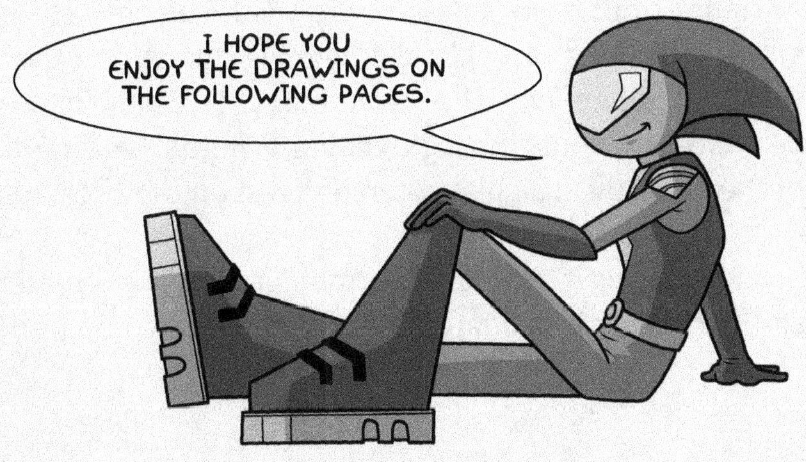

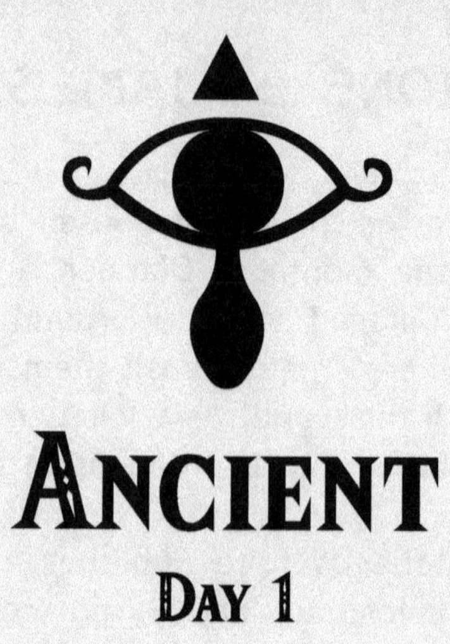

ANCIENT
DAY 1

Linktober kicked off with a very interesting prompt. It wasn't a name of a character, location, or weapon, which would be easy to conceptualize. Ancient requires the use of creativity right out of the box. I welcomed the challenge.

The world of Hyrule spans hundreds, if not, thousands of years. Relatively speaking, anything relating to the early games on the Zelda Timeline would qualify as "ancient". Even the first game in the series, *Skyward Sword*, alludes to a pre-history of war and strife. Locations are littered with evidence of civilizations long gone. Ruins and ancient robots are just a few examples.

Instead, I chose to illustrate the hero, Link, wearing the Ancient Armor from *Breath of the Wild*. This set, which includes greaves, upper apparel, and a helm, is styled after the terrifying Guardian enemies. The technology is Sheikah, which can be made obvious through their perpetual use of their "Eye of the Sheikah" insignia as can be seen on the breastplate.

Wearing the ancient armor grants Link greater offense stat boosts against Guardian enemies. A welcome perk!

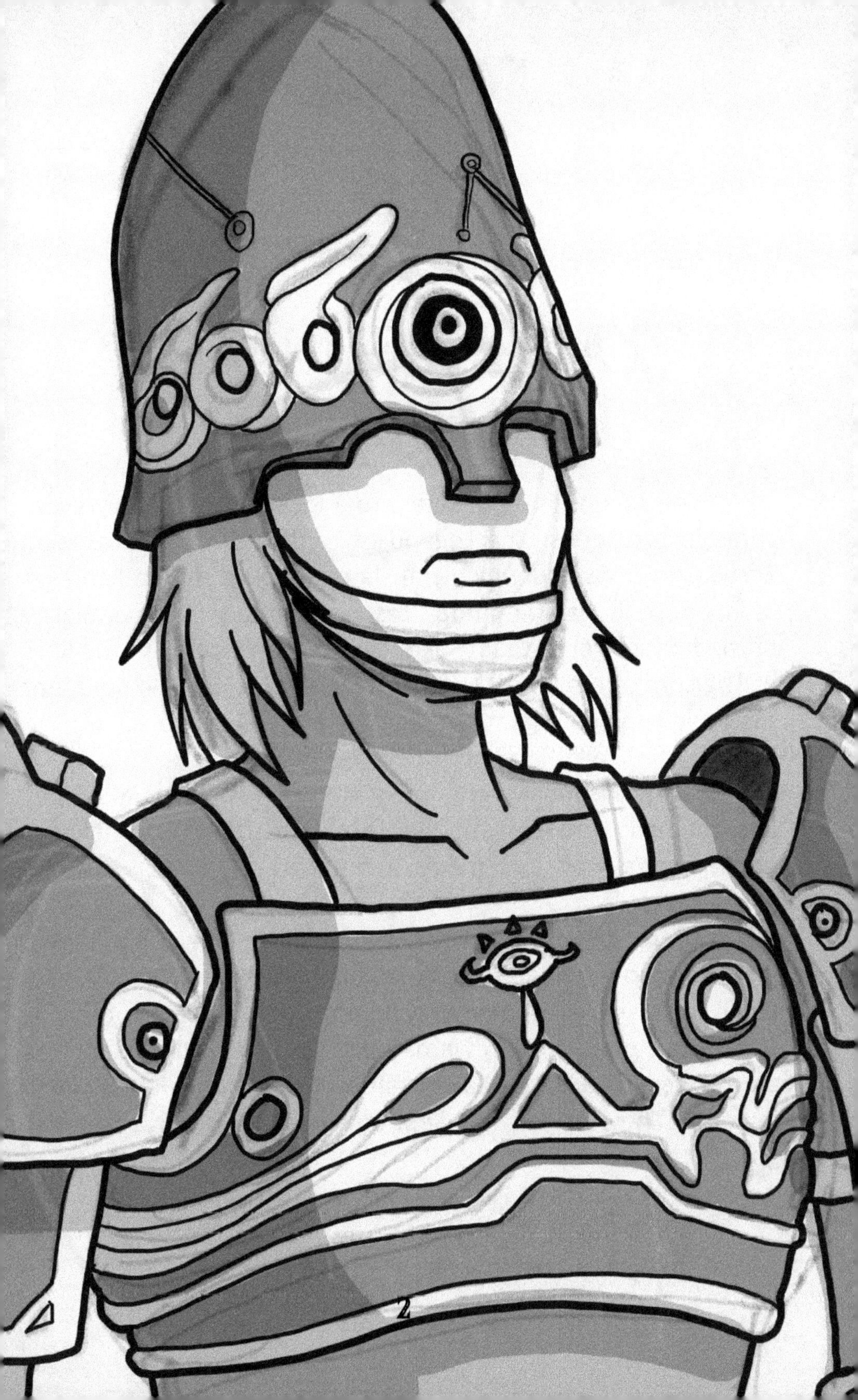

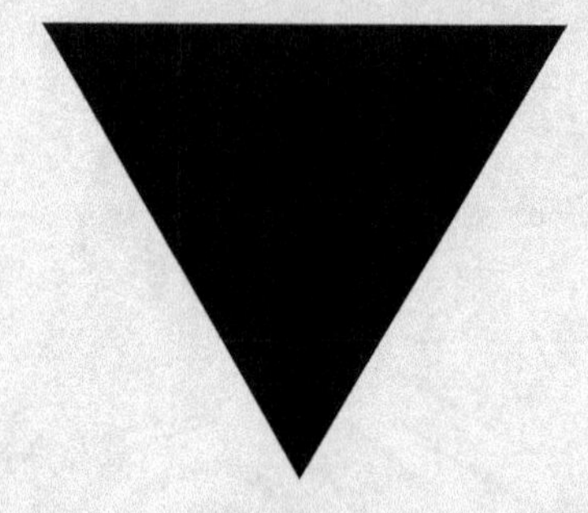

FAIRY FOUNTAIN
DAY 2

The second prompt refers to a location in virtually every game in the series. The Legend of Zelda was originally called *Zeruda no Densetsu* which translates to "The Hyrule Fantasy" in Japanese. It was Nintendo's response to the rising popularity of the fantasy genre that took the world by storm with the likes of *The Lord of the Rings*, *The Chronicles of Narnia*, and no doubt the table-top board game series, *Dungeons & Dragons*.

As with most other fantasy worlds, certain tropes and themes were present per the standard. These included elves, castles, monsters, magic, and of course, fairies.

There are several types of fairies in the Zelda series, including the guardian fairies, healing fairies, and Great Fairies. Fairy Fountains are commonly hidden and therefore difficult to find but offer great rewards upon visiting. They are almost always occupied with healing fairies to soothe Link's wounds in battle. They can even be kept in a glass bottle for aid on the go.

Fairies come in all shapes and sizes depending on the style of the game they appear in.

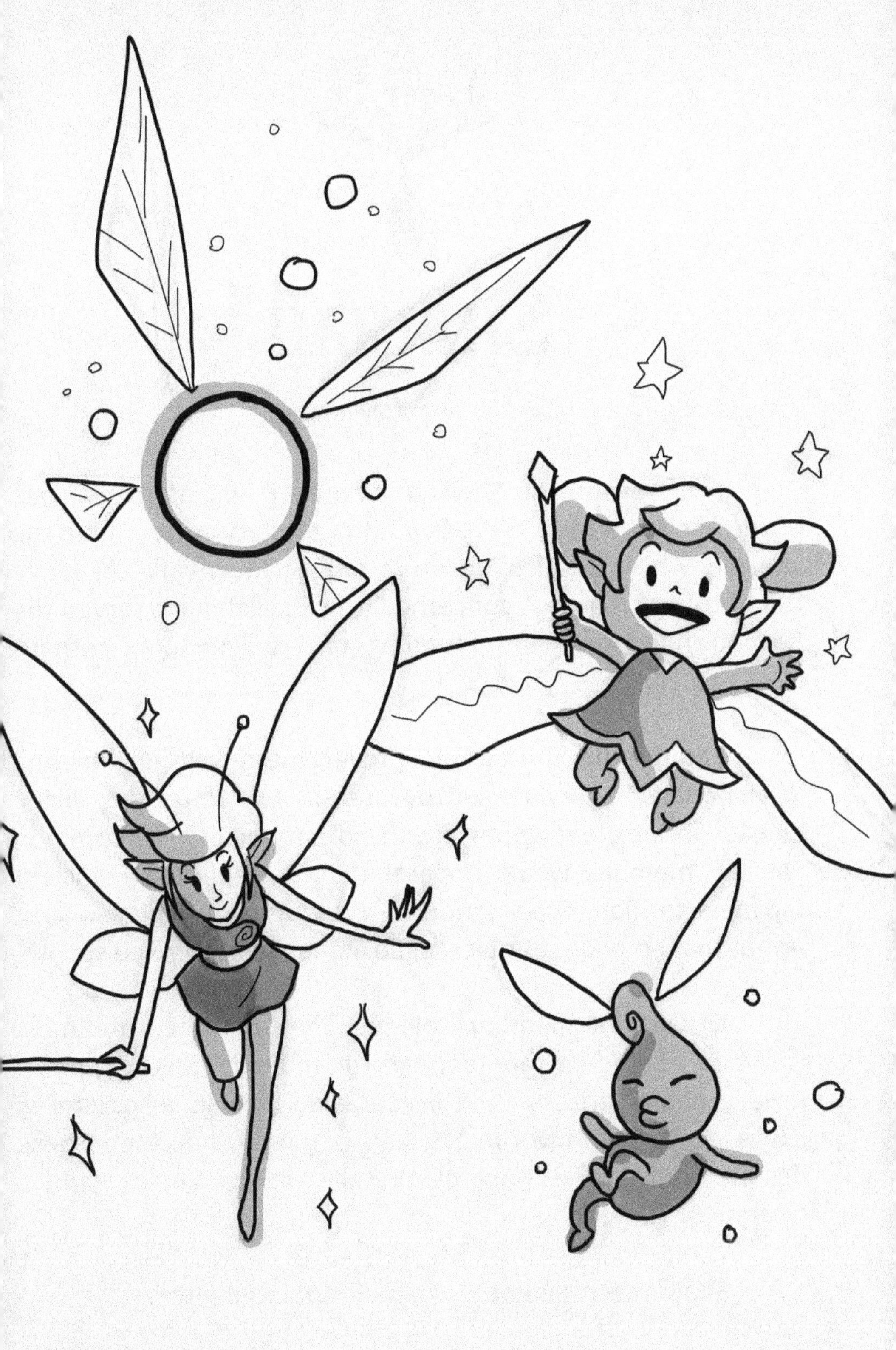

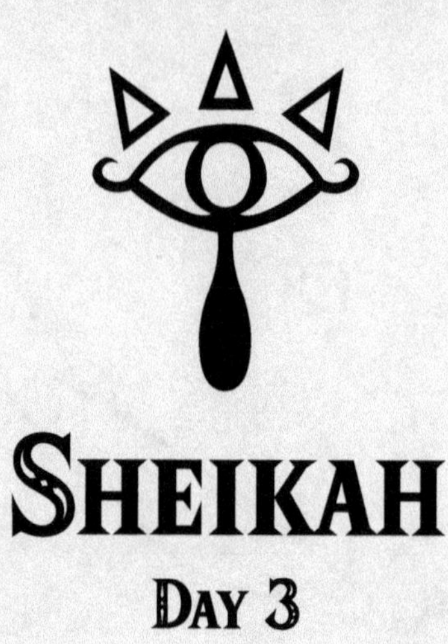

SHEIKAH
DAY 3

I referenced the Sheikah tribe on Day 1 as the makers of the ancient armor. There is a lot of mystery surrounding the Sheikah, which are also known as the "Shadow Folk". As far as the history of Hyrule is concerned, the Sheikah have served the Royal Family since the founding of the kingdom, perhaps even earlier.

Though the Sheikah are proven masters in engineering & technology, as evidenced by the Sheikah Slate, the Divine Beasts, Shrines, and other advanced antiquities, the common Sheikah member wears apparel that is inspired by ancient Japanese fashion. The warriors garb themselves in light-weight armor that emphasizes quick, agile maneuverability and stealth.

Of all the members of the Sheikah tribe, the most common character that appears in multiple titles is Impa, usually characterized as Princess Zelda's personal caretaker. However, the fan-favorite Sheikah is none other than Sheik, despite only appearing canonically in a single game... *Ocarina of Time*.

Sheik's secret identity is a major point of interest.

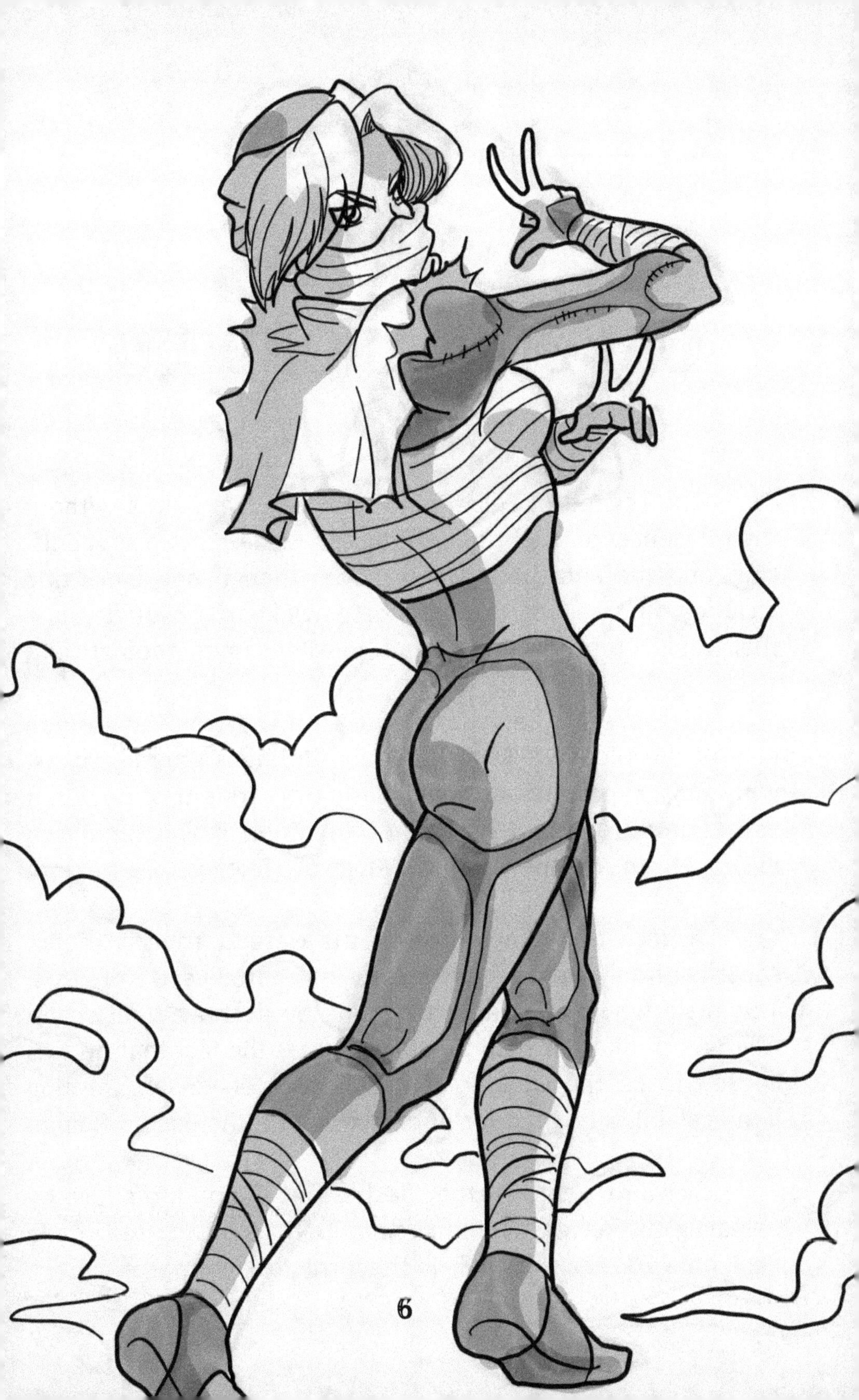

GANON/GANONDORF
DAY 4

The Legend of Zelda would not be what is it is without the presence of the titular Princess Zelda, the protagonist Link, and the antagonist Ganon. Even though not every title includes all three of these Triforce wielders, I would argue that their presence is still felt in the games thematically.

In the early depictions of Ganon, he was the Demon King of the Moblins. Ganon was an enormous boar-like beast with magical powers and fought using the trident of power. It wasn't until *Ocarina of Time* that Ganon's origin was canonized in the form of the Gerudo King of Thieves, Ganondorf.

A peculiar characteristic of the Gerudo Tribe is that it consists of only women, but one male is born every 100 years. This male would be made their king by decree. What made Ganondorf different than previous kings is the fact that he was chosen to be the wielder of the Triforce of Power, granting him the ability to conquer both Hyrule and the Sacred Realm.

Skyward Sword further fleshes out Ganondorf's lore by revealing the never-ending curse of Demise, his hatred made flesh time and again, usually in the form of Ganondorf.

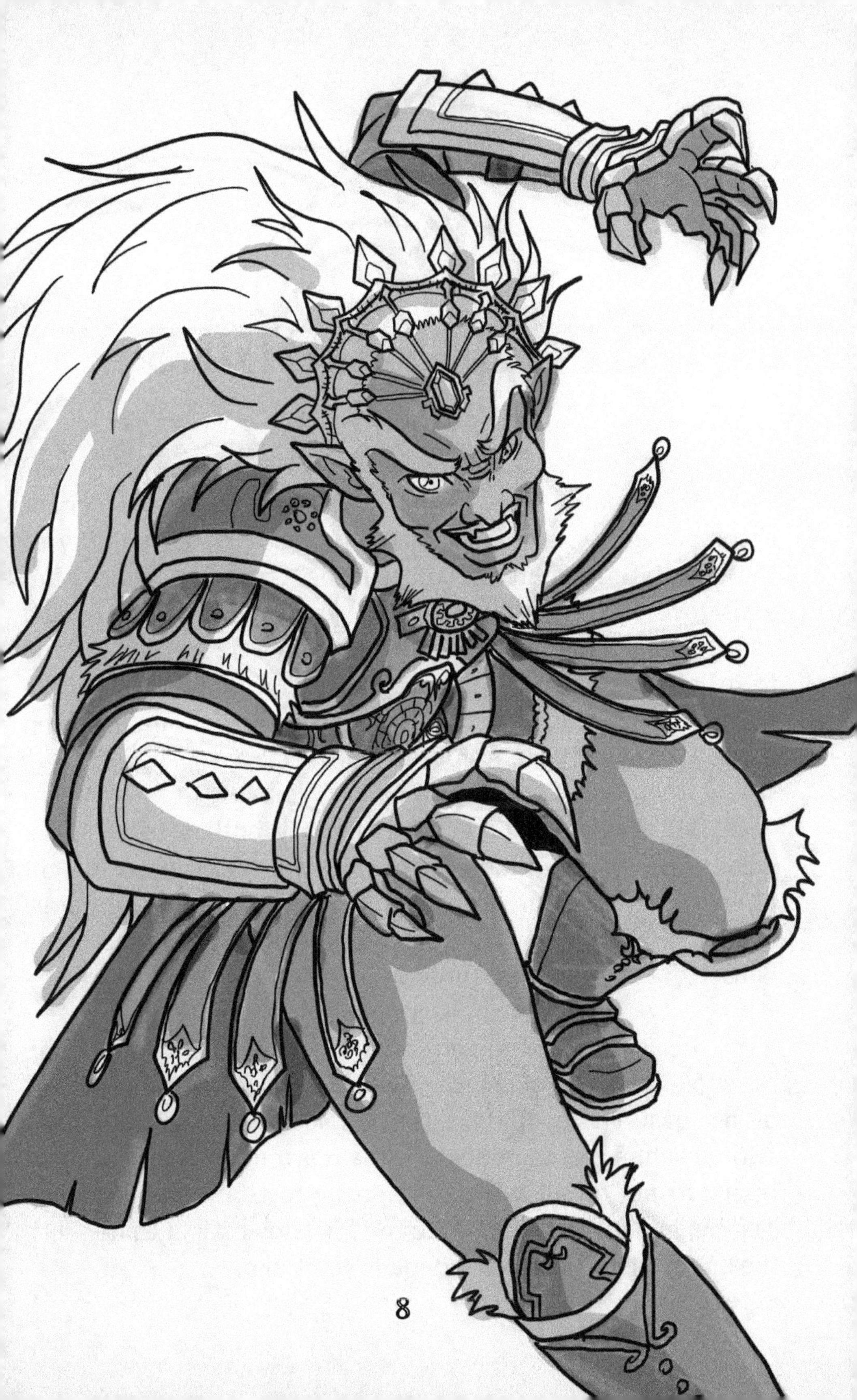

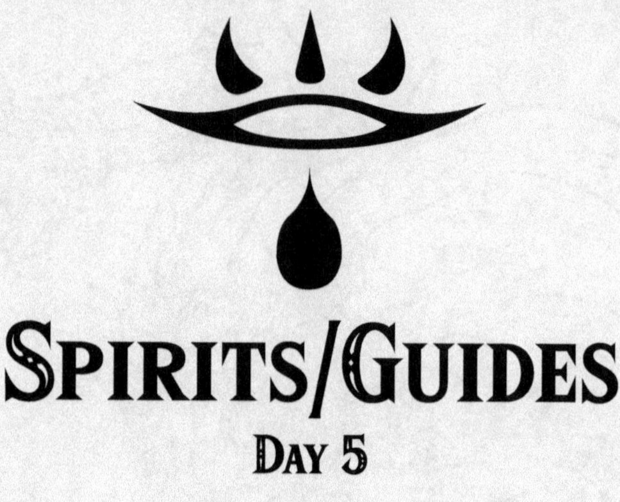

SPIRITS/GUIDES
DAY 5

In virtually every game in the series, Link is either accompanied by a helpful guide throughout the majority of the adventure or meets reoccurring characters who offer assistance to Link, and to the player by proxy. These would vary from supporting characters who offer aid in the form of side-quests, item upgrades, or directional advice to the spirits who watch from a distance but are invested in the actions of the hero for more altruistic purposes.

My favorite spirit guide is literally both a spirit and a guide. The Hero's Shade makes his appearance in *Twilight Princess*. Though the form he takes is that of an ethereal Stalfos, his actual identity is none other than the Hero of Time himself, from *Ocarina of Time*.

Twilight Princess Link is a direct descendant of the Hero of Time. As such, the Hero's Shade eases the regret of his past life by passing on his knowledge of advanced sword fighting techniques to the current hero. Leaving a legacy to his kin allows him to finally rest in peace, knowing that he, in part, was integral to the final downfall of Ganondorf, the enemy he once thwarted many years ago.

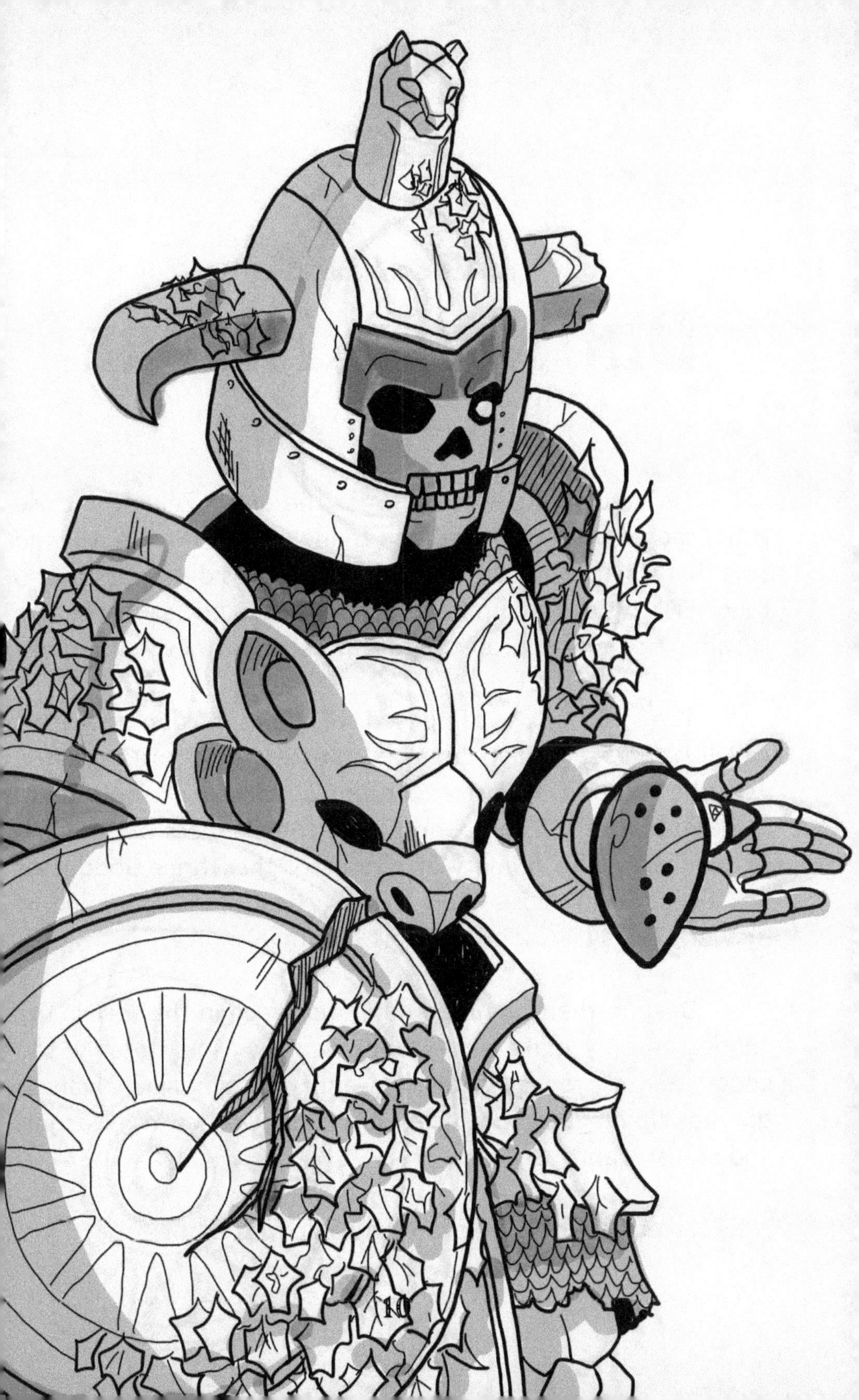

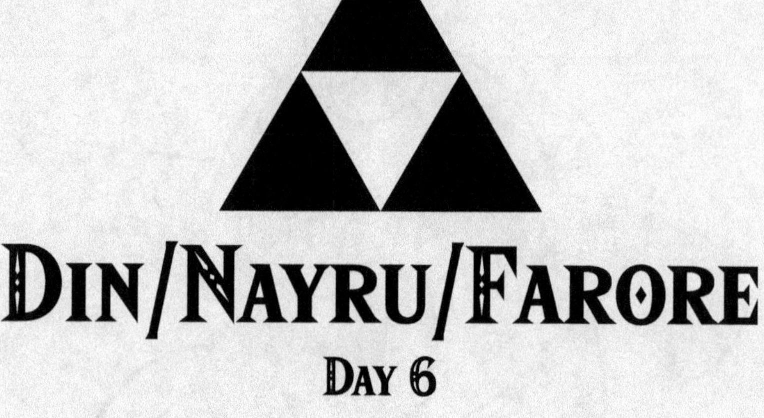

Din/Nayru/Farore
Day 6

The underlying MacGuffin for the entire Zelda franchise is the sacred objects, the golden triangles: the Triforce. Legend says that it has the power to grant the heart's desire of he who touches it. It's easy to understand why such a powerful treasure is something worth protecting from those with evil intentions.

The Triforce is composed of three golden triangles, which represent the Three Goddesses who are credited with the creation of Hyrule: Din the Goddess of Power, Nayru the Goddess of Wisdom, and Farore the Goddess of Courage. By extension, the primary attributes of the Three Goddesses are exhibited in those chosen by destiny, namely Ganondorf (Power), Zelda (Wisdom) and Link (Courage).

Despite their monumental importance in the series, the goddesses only make a few appearances. Most notably, the goddesses take on physical form and walk among mortals in the handheld games: *Oracles of Ages*, *Oracles of Seasons*, and *Minish Cap*.

I would love to see them return in future titles!

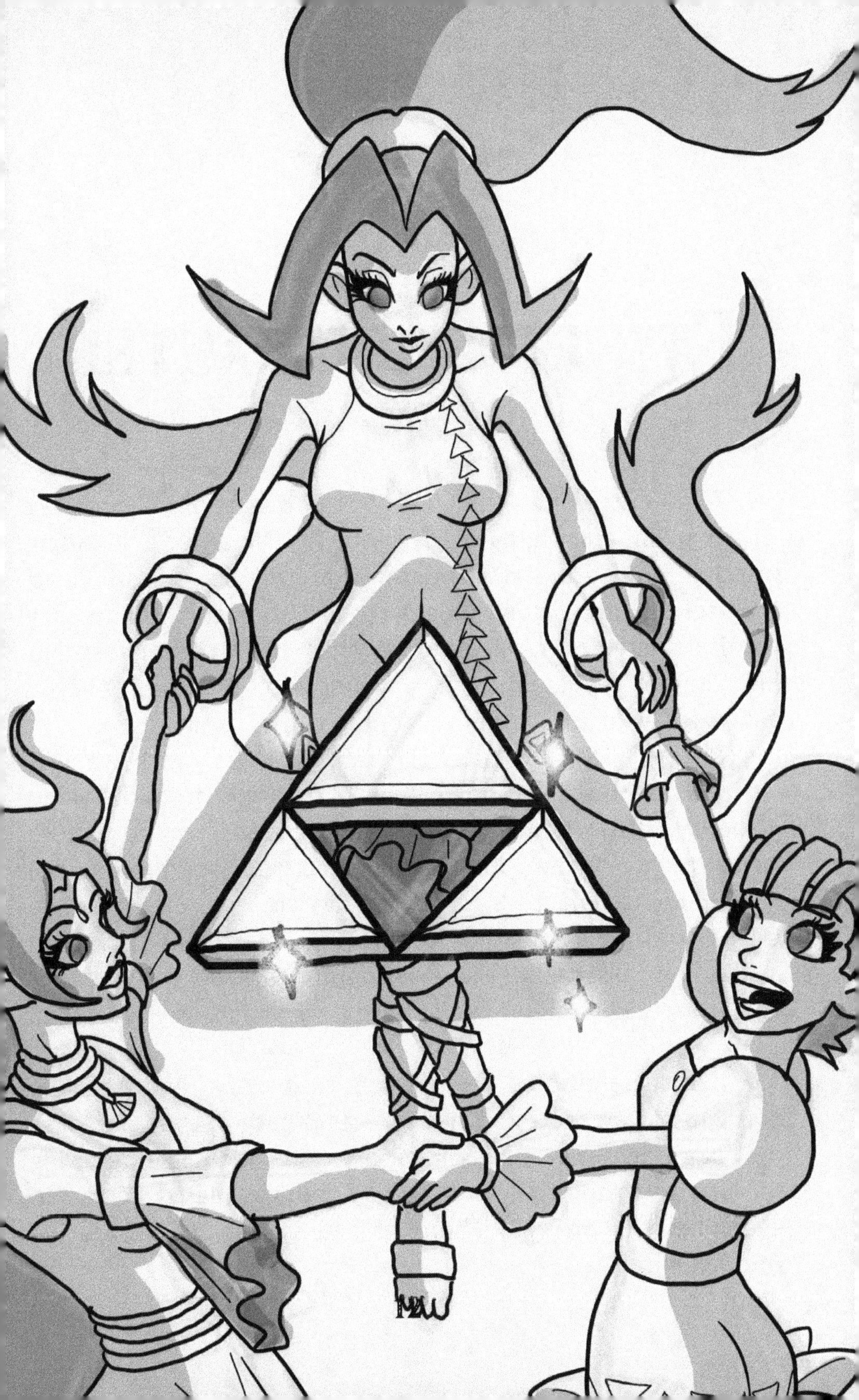

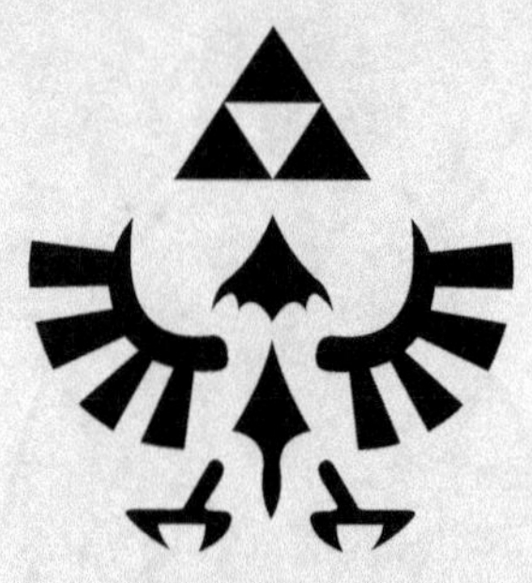

Favorite Character
Day 7

I'm not alone when I say that my favorite character is the main man himself: Link. It was Nintendo's founding principle to feature a character that the player can insert themselves into, virtually speaking, like an avatar. That is why Link is depicted as the silent protagonist. It's my best guess that his common appearance as a young, soft-featured, elf-type allows for even lady gamer to identify with.

I know first-hand how powerful the "link" from the video game world to my own had on my childhood psyche. Before virtual reality or the robust character creator seen in modern games, controlling Link for the first time in a 3D Hyrule in *Ocarina of Time* has seared into the minds of millions of children in the late 90's, creating lasting memories filled with wonder and adventure. Nintendo definitely knew what they were doing.

Zelda promotes exploration, discovery, and creative problem-solving. Later entries such as Breath of the Wild takes that approach and applies it on a world-wide scale, allowing the players to tell their own tale of courage that is unique to everyone. Link may the hero of the series, but so are we through him!

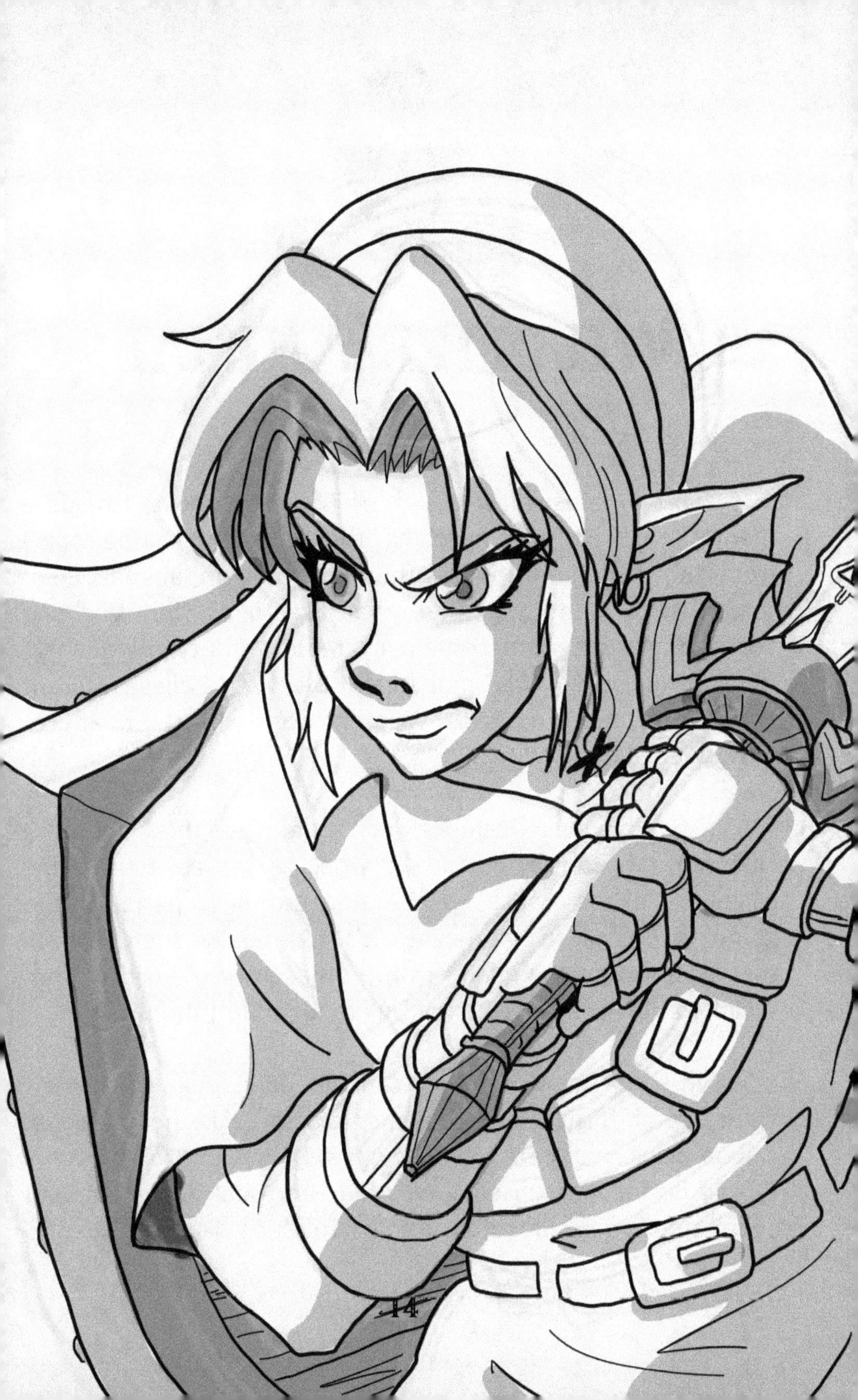

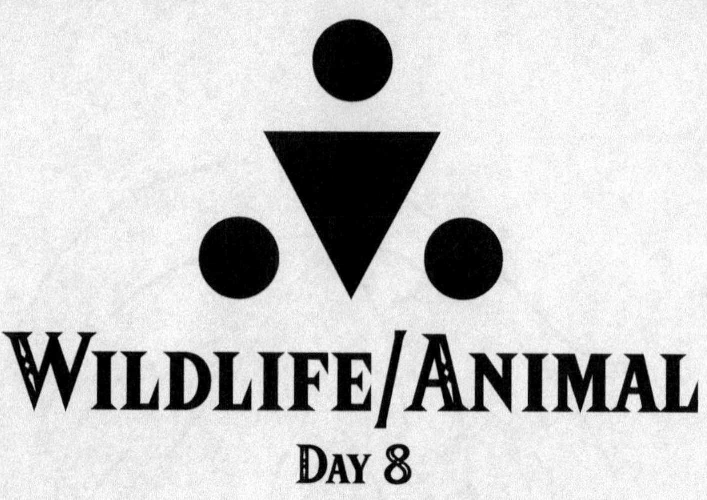

WILDLIFE/ANIMAL
DAY 8

On my latest playthrough of *Twilight Princess* I made a mental note about something that sets this game apart from the rest, and that is the emphasis on animals/creatures. There is no argument that *Breath of the Wild* and *Tears of the Kingdom* contain a greater variety of fauna in the form of wildlife and monsters. However, I believe *Twilight Princess* has more noteworthy interactions with the creatures of Hyrule.

The obvious instance of course is the fact that Link himself transforms into a wolf, so far as even being called a "divine beast". While not the best parts of the game in terms of gameplay, it's essentially the gimmick that differentiates itself from other titles, aside from *A Link to the Past* (does Bunny Link really count, though?).

In the game the player can not only speak to animals while in wolf form, but herd goats, care for Link's horse Epona, call on hawks, cooperate with monkeys, buy lantern oil from a talking bird, collect insects, play hide-and-seek with cats, and even temporarily control a Cucco (Hyrule's chicken equivalent)!

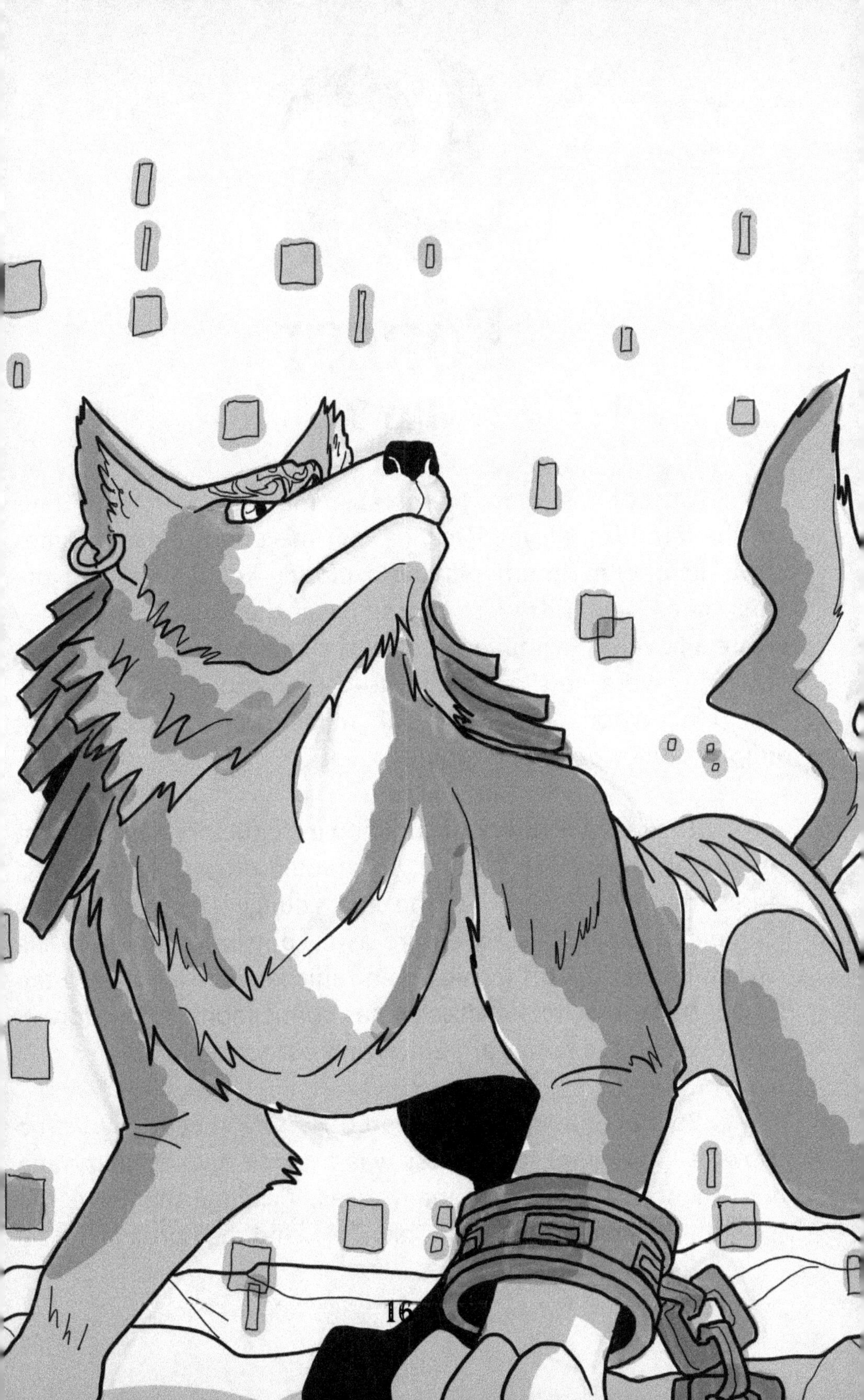

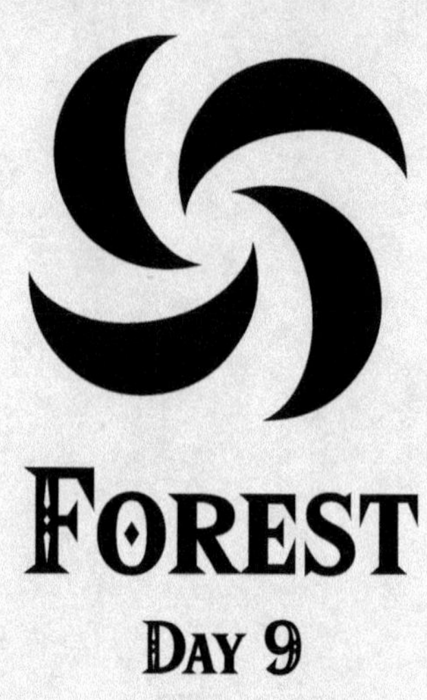

FOREST

DAY 9

One of the most memorable moments for many fans in the late 90's, playing Ocarina of Time upon release, comes from its opening moments and exploring Kokiri Forest for the first time. 3D worlds were impressive at the time because they were a novelty. Swimming in creeks, climbing trees, and scaling cliffsides were new mechanics for players to enjoy. Exploring the Lost Woods as Young Link made such a positive first impression I won't soon forget.

The forest is the most common introductory environment in virtually every Zelda game. This would often also include a forest-themed temple as the first dungeon as well. Link commonly begins his adventure as an outsider, despite being Hylian by blood. This iconic green tunic lends itself well to the visual trope that this character has connections to the forest, where elves and fairies are universally associated with.

Before Ganondorf conquered Hyrule (specifically in the Downfall Timeline), the forest was a place of tranquility and life. The forest is home to many races, including the Kikwi, the Minish, the Kokiri, the Great Deku Tree, and the Koroks.

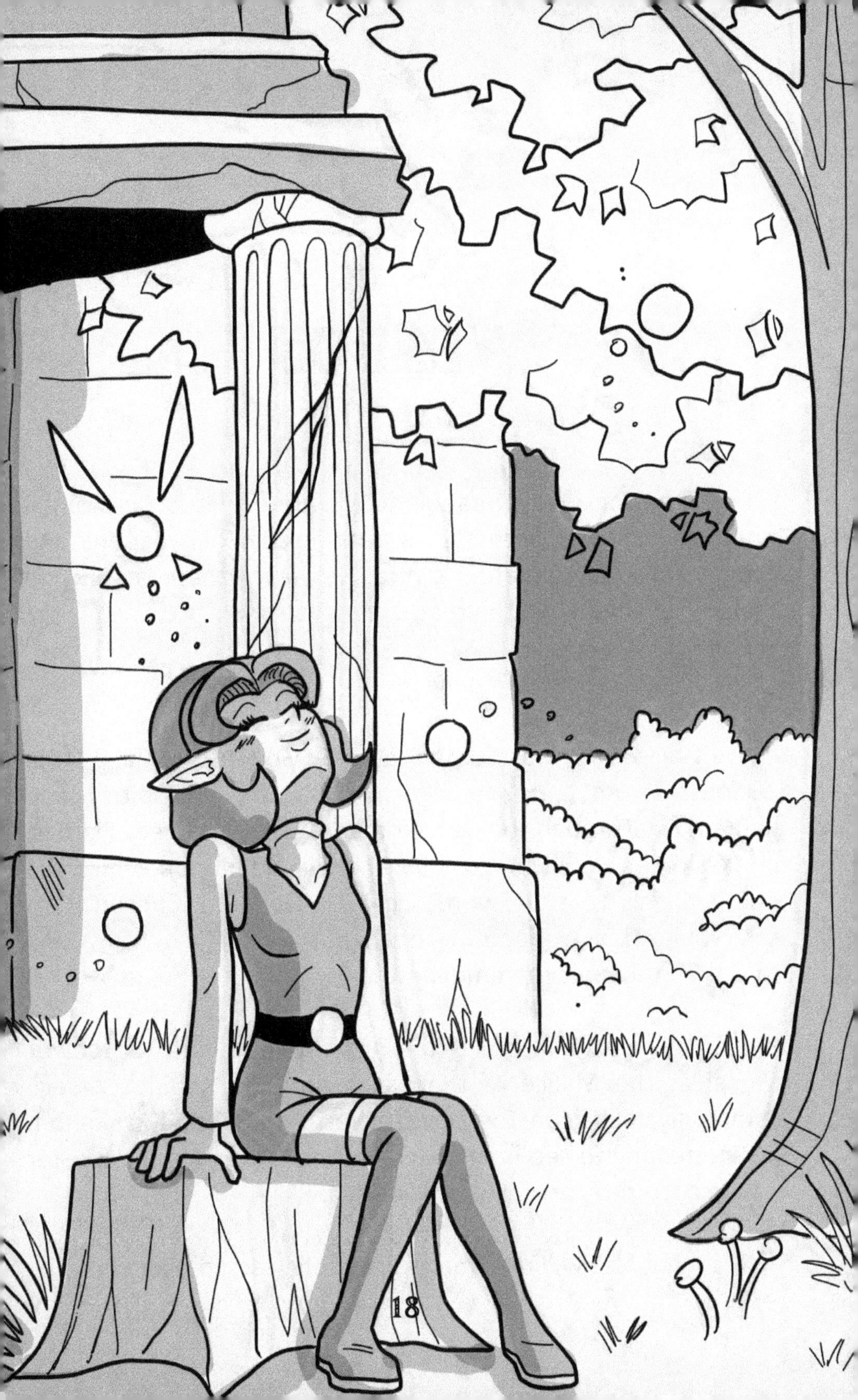

18

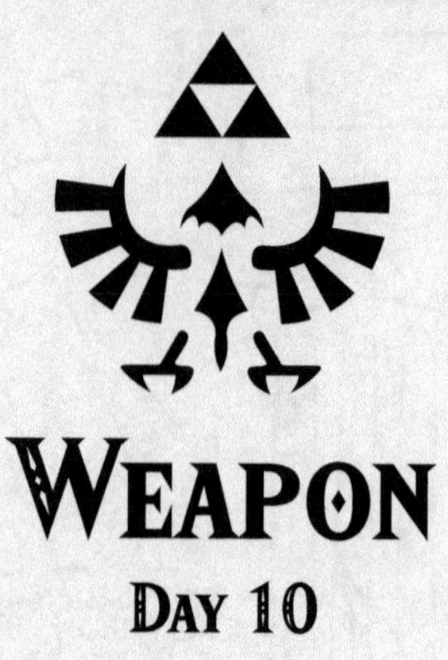

WEAPON
DAY 10

Choosing what weapon to illustrate was a no-brainer. Although Link has access to a vast arsenal of weapons and gadgets, including different swords. However, there is only one that stands out above the rest.

The Blade of Evil's Bane.

The sword was forged by the Goddess Hylia as the Goddess Sword and given life in the form of a spirit guide named Fi. Through being reforged by the Sacred Flames, it takes on its iconic indigo color and winged hilt, becoming the one and only Master Sword. Only the Goddess' Chosen Hero can wield this weapon, a title that passes on from Link to Link throughout the timelines.

The Master Sword is the only weapon with the power to defeat the Malice of Demise, a persistent source of evil commonly taking on the physical form of Ganondorf/Ganon. It's interesting to see how in *Tears of the Kingdom*, the Master Sword becomes corrupted and inert.

What fate will become of Fi and the sacred blade?

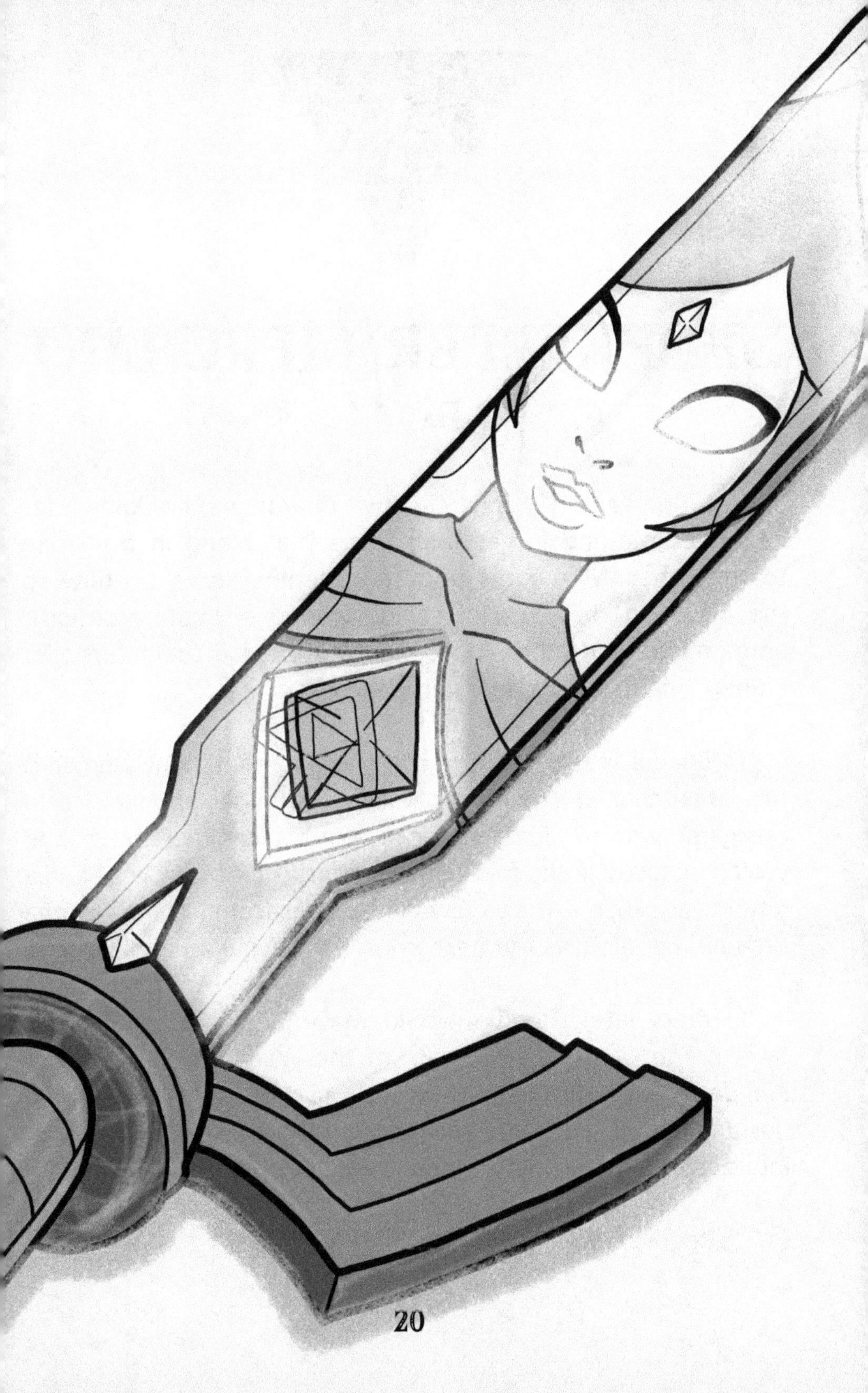

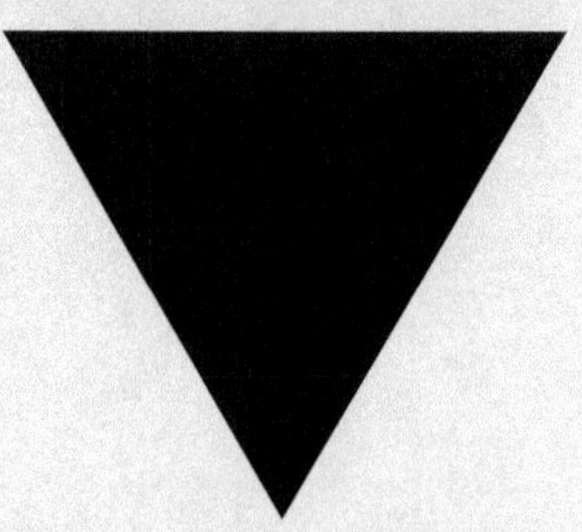

SHOPKEEPER/MERCHANT
DAY 11

Video game NPCs (Non-Player Characters) are known for being generic and forgettable; Faces that blend in from one to the other. Merchants and shopkeepers serve a utility to the player in the form of selling weapons, healing potions, ammunition, and other goods. Rarely are these characters ever named, and rarely do they persist across games.

Beedle is the name of the traveling merchant who sails the Great Sea in *The Wind Waker*. His initial appearance in this game was a milestone because of his iconic greetings and voiced dialogue in the form of an enthusiastic "thank you" and a bittersweet "bye". After a few voiced lines from Navi in *Ocarina of Time*, Beedle was the next in line for having an audible role.

Years later, Beedle would make a return in *Skyward Sword*, *The Minish Cap*, *Breath of the Wild*, and *Tears of the Kingdom*. Each new game expands his role and personality, fleshing out his backstory and incorporating more ways you can interact with him aside from purchasing his wares.

Beedle is well-deserving of today's feature.

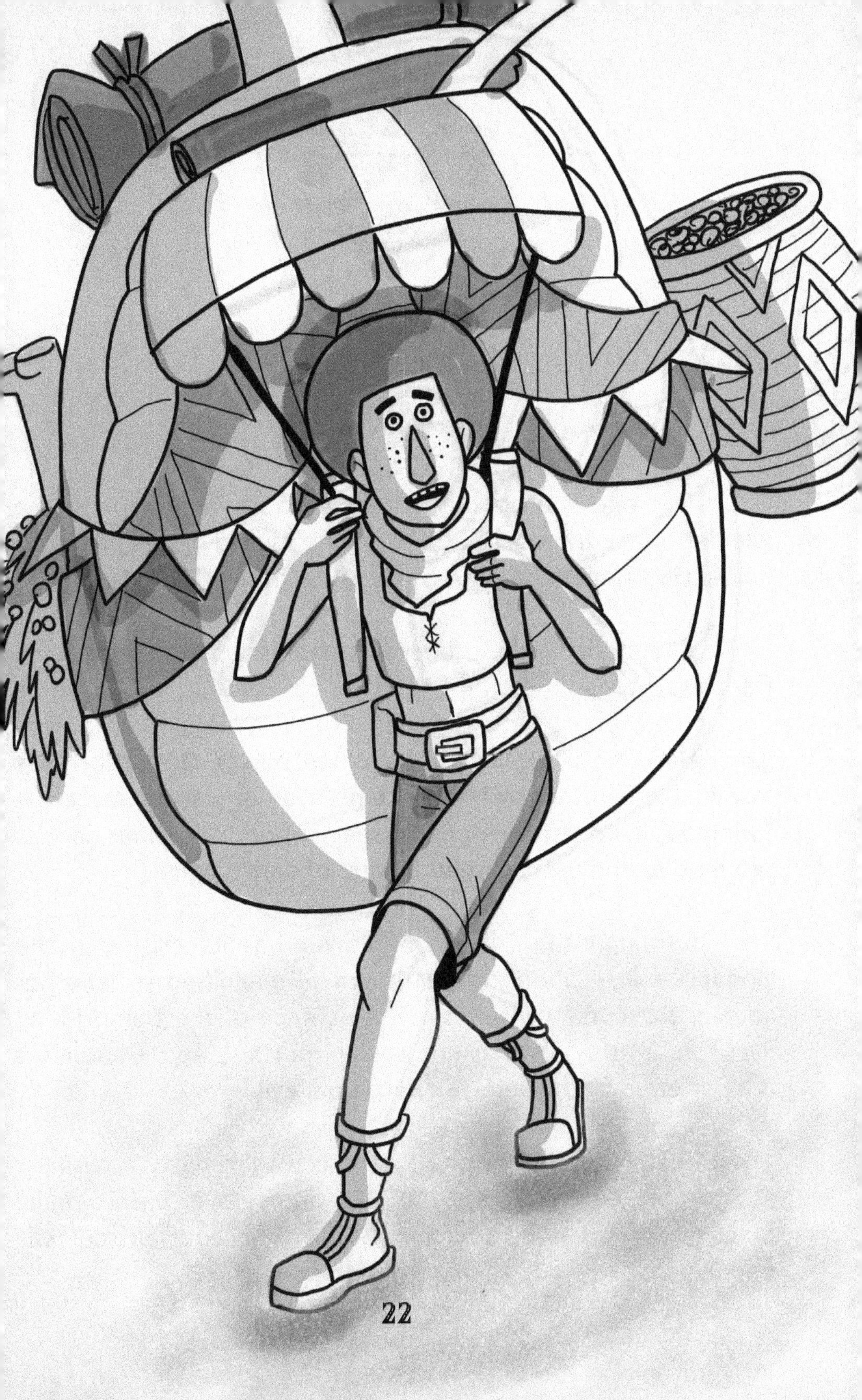

POWER

DAY 12

This one is a double feature because Ganondorf is the wielder of the Triforce of Power and he's wielding the infamous Power Glove, made famous by the 1989 movie *The Wizard*.

Ganondorf is the primary antagonist of the entire Zelda franchise. He's the third entity, completing the Triforce personified, along with Link and Princess Zelda. Even before gaining access to the Goddess' golden power, Ganondorf was formidable in his own right. Since his mother was the sorceress Twinrova, it's no stretch of the imagination to assume he was brought up and proficient in the arts of dark magic.

Although the Triforce of Power has its origins in the Goddess Din, Ganondorf's strength is magnified by another source: the curse of Demise. The essence of the Demon King lives on in the form of powerful mortals, and Ganondorf is a perfect host for Demise's perpetual evil.

The Nintendo Power Glove was a third-party accessory, a wearable controller for the NES. The glove wasn't really practical and barely functional, but the cool factor was undeniable. **Now you're playing with power!**

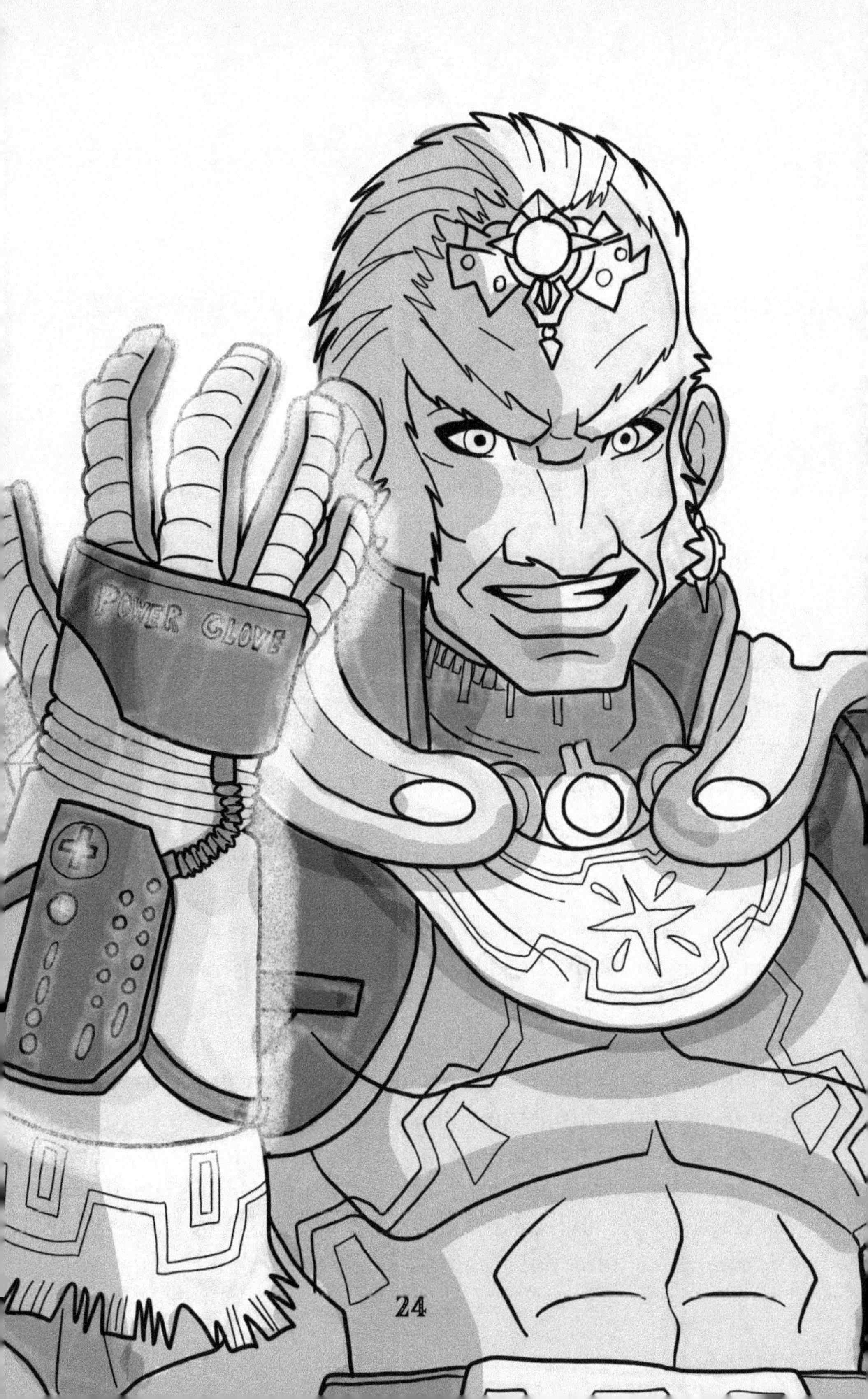

POWER GLOVE
24

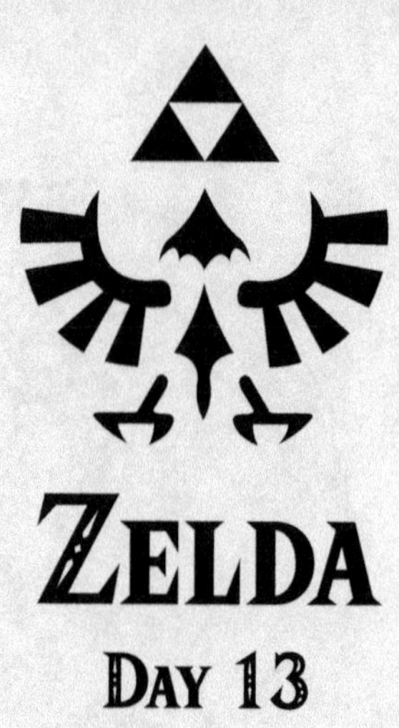

ZELDA

Day 13

Although the prompt for the day was pretty straight forward, there was actually quite a lot of room for creativity, given the fact that the name of Zelda was given to every princess in Hyrule's history. I could have picked from more than a dozen different princesses to illustrate, but I was inspired to depict her as seen in *Breath of the Wild* because I love her casual outdoor attire.

Zelda is typically wearing elegant dresses, as is proper for royalty. There are a few instances where her character is wearing pants, but they are typically reserved for disguises. *Breath of the Wild* introduces a princess who wanders Hyrule; A people's princess, if you will. She is scholarly with a peculiar interest in Sheikah technology and history.

Another possible reason why she resonates with a lot of fans today is because, thanks to modern improvements in storytelling in video games, this Zelda is the most well-rounded princess when compared to her other counterparts. She experiences significant character growth, trails & challenges, and agency as she takes on an active role in saving Hyrule, experiencing more loss and sacrifice than the average Zelda.

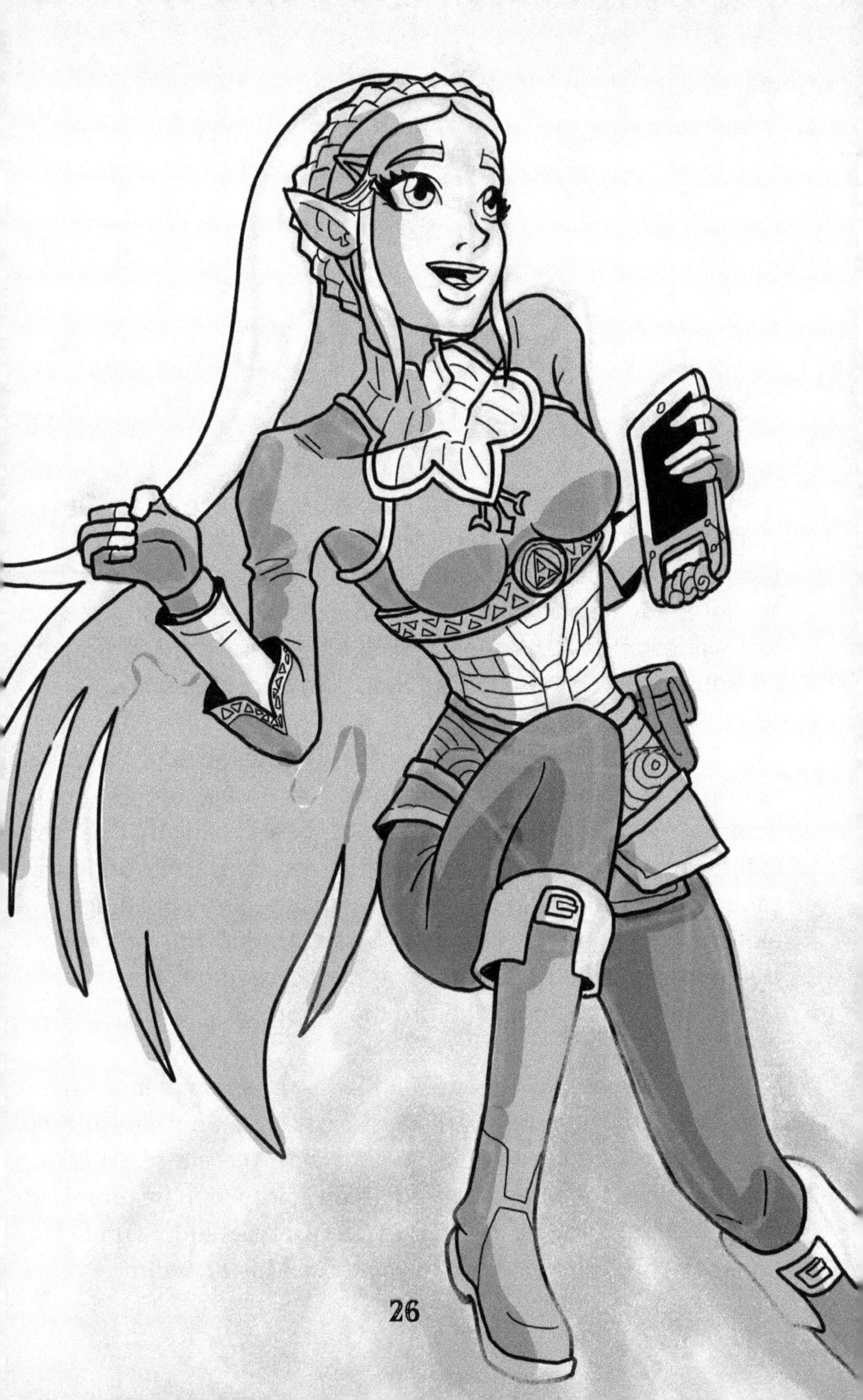

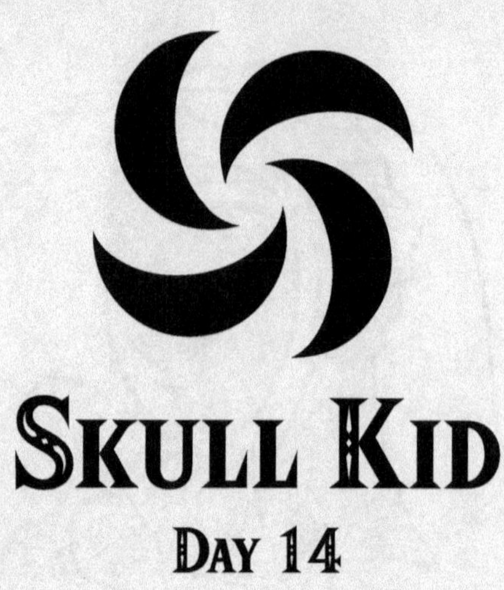

Skull Kid

Day 14

Skull Kid refers to both a type of over-world "monster" as well as the name given to a very specific Skull Kid that Link interacts with on multiple occasions. According to the lore, any Kokiri child that wanders into the forest and gets lost will eventually become a Skull Kid. There is a counterpart for adults who become lost as well, they become Stalfos.

The Skull Kid made his first appearance in *Ocarina of Time,* in which Link befriends him using Saria's Song. Link is rewarded with a piece of heart and that is the extent of his relevance in that game. It wasn't until the sequel, where Skull Kid is given the expanded role of antagonist alongside the titular *Majora's Mask.* Under the control of the mask, Skull Kid becomes a public menace and Link is tasked with stopping him before the Moon falls.

Link eventually saves Skull Kid by reminding him of their friendship but then they part ways. Years later, another Link will find his way through the Lost Woods with the aid of Skull Kid, who has since then become a guardian spirit when he promised to keep the entrance to the Sacred Grove hidden until the time came for the next hero to wield the Master Sword.

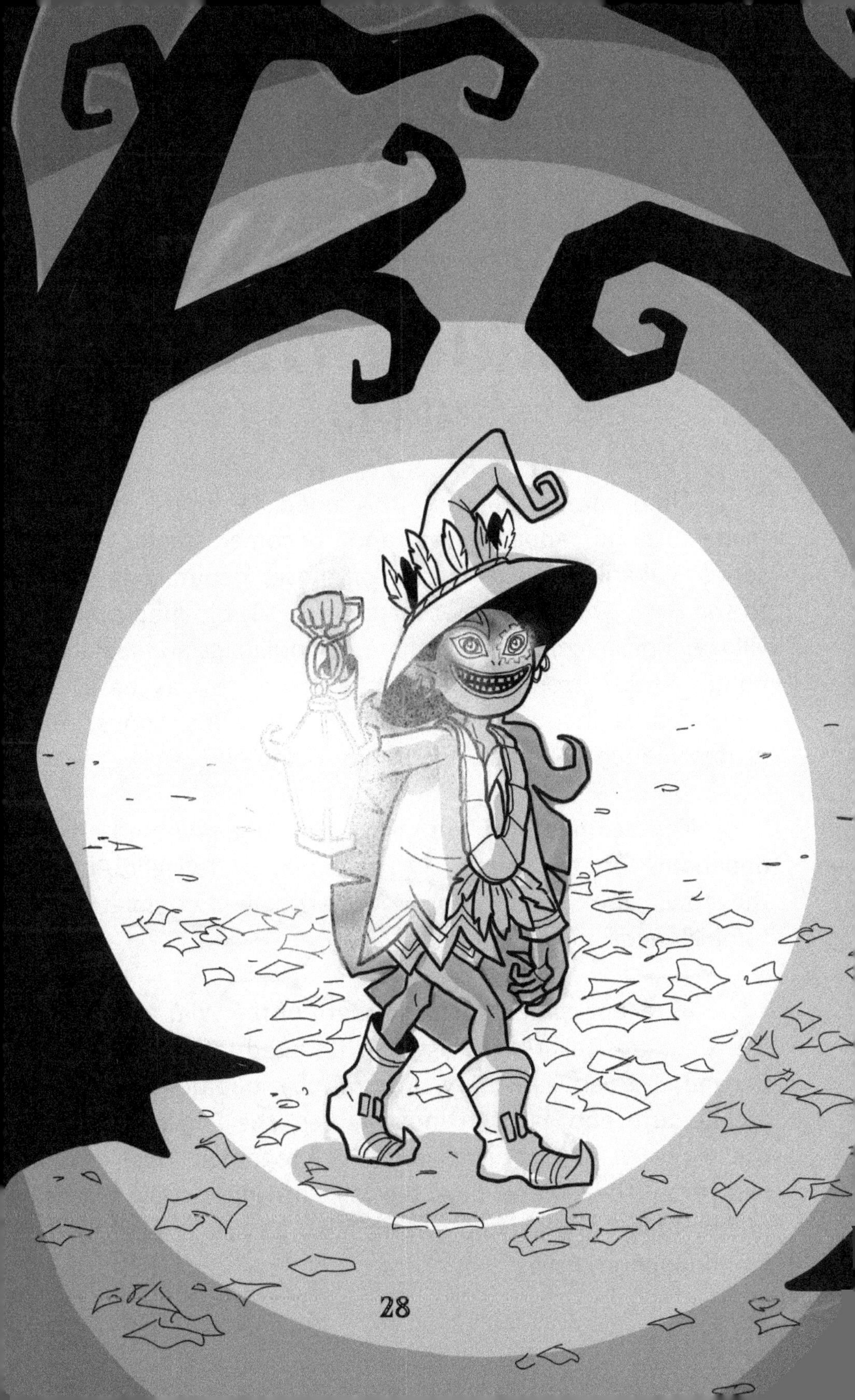

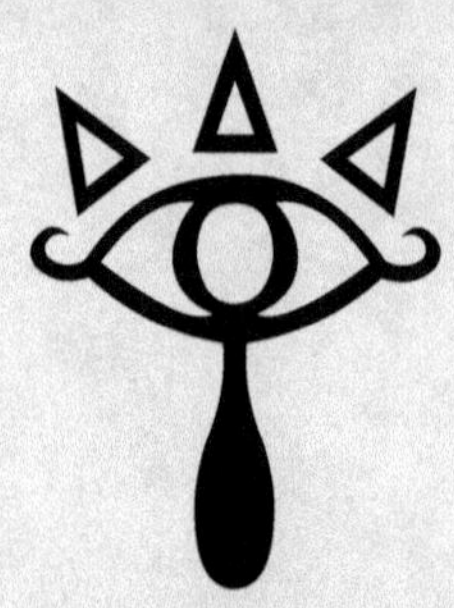

KAKARIKO VILLAGE
DAY 15

There are a handful of named locations that have made several appearances and become staples in the series. Kakariko Village is one of these, debuting in *A Link to the Past*. The small town began as a classic medieval-style village, a place containing commercial buildings and residential homes. Aside from Hyrule Castle town, it was easily the liveliest area in the game, bustling with NPCs, shops, mini-games, hidden treasures, and optional side-quests.

The aesthetics of the village would evolve and change depending on the game. For example, in *Twilight Princess* the town took on a more Western vibe, complete with tumbleweeds and bandit raids.

In recent games, such as *Breath of the Wild* and *Tears of the Kingdom*, Kakariko Village was updated to become a fully-fledged Sheikah sanctuary, inspired by traditional Japanese architecture and garb. In most games, the Sheikah were on the verge of extinction or missing altogether. This was the first time they were depicted as thriving people. Initially under Impa's leadership, eventually passed down to her granddaughter, Paya.

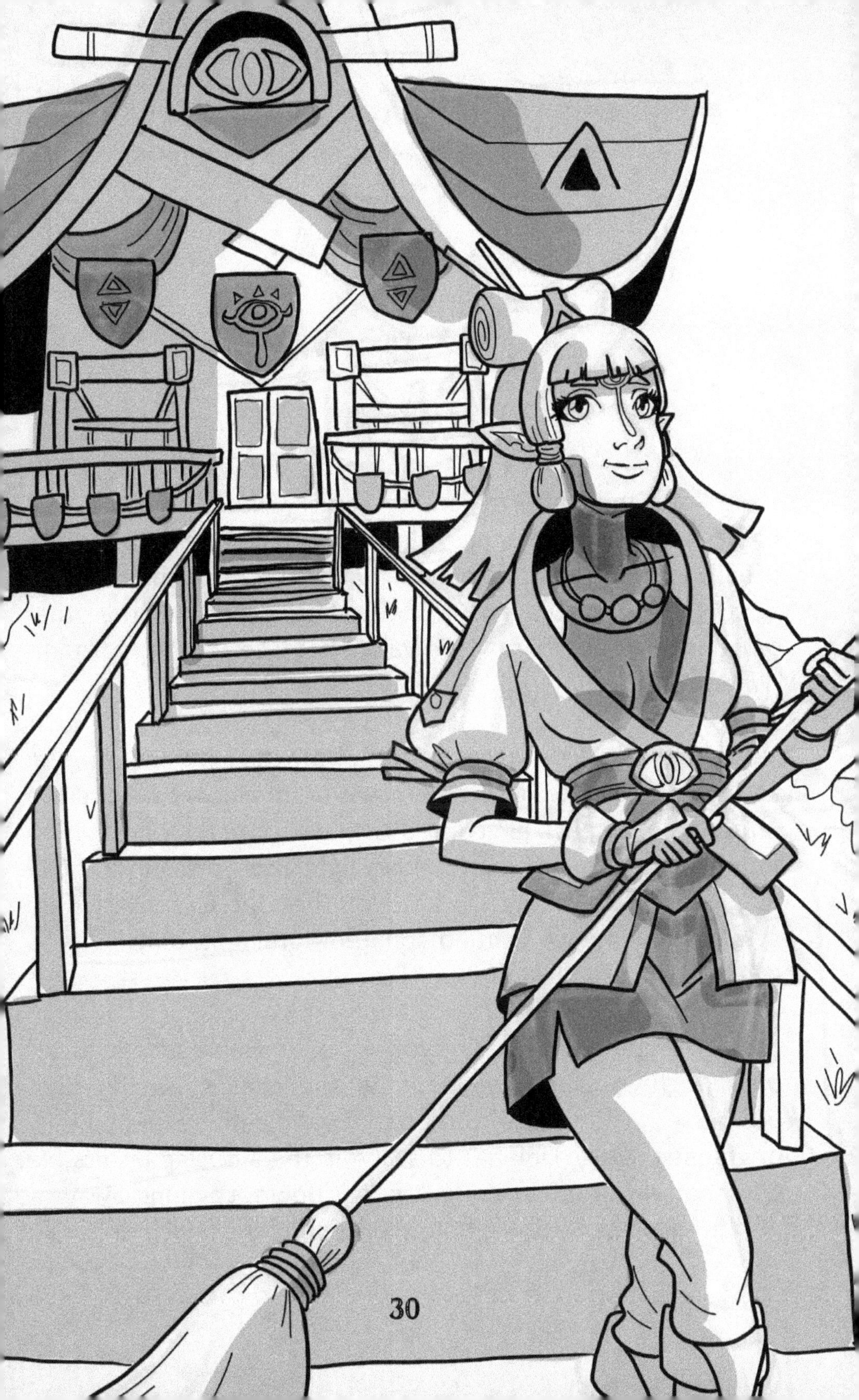

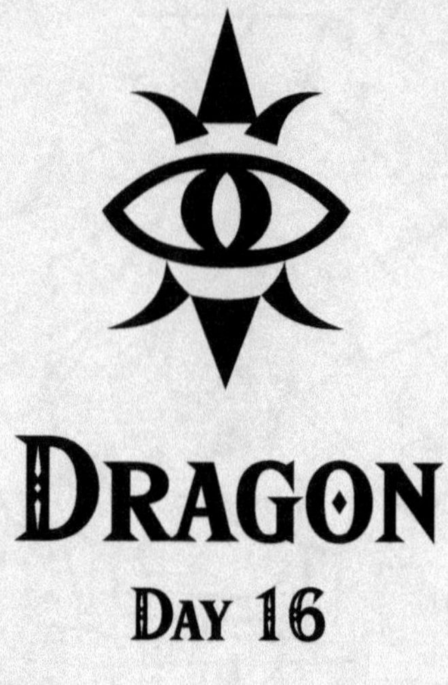

DRAGON
DAY 16

As a foundational fantasy series, *The Legend of Zelda* has its fair share of dragons in almost every game in the series, usually in the form of a boss. In *Twilight Princess*, the dungeon boss is the Twilit Dragon, Argorok. I chose him over the other dragons such as Volvagia or Valoo because I love its armor-plated design.

Argorok is a wyvern, a type of dragon that has wings in lieu of arms, and two legs. This makes them much more bird-like rather than simply a large lizard with wings on their back. It's a fitting choice considering the boss fight takes place in the City in the Sky, where the Oocca live. The Oocca, similarly, are avian in appearance with no apparent forelimbs, only legs and wings.

The battle with Argorok is very cinematic. It takes place high in the sky, hidden in the clouds. As the fight progresses, the clouds turn dark and lightning periodically brightens the sky. Link has to swing in the air using his double Clawshots in order to bring Argorok down, chipping away as his armor, piece by piece, before delivering the final blow.

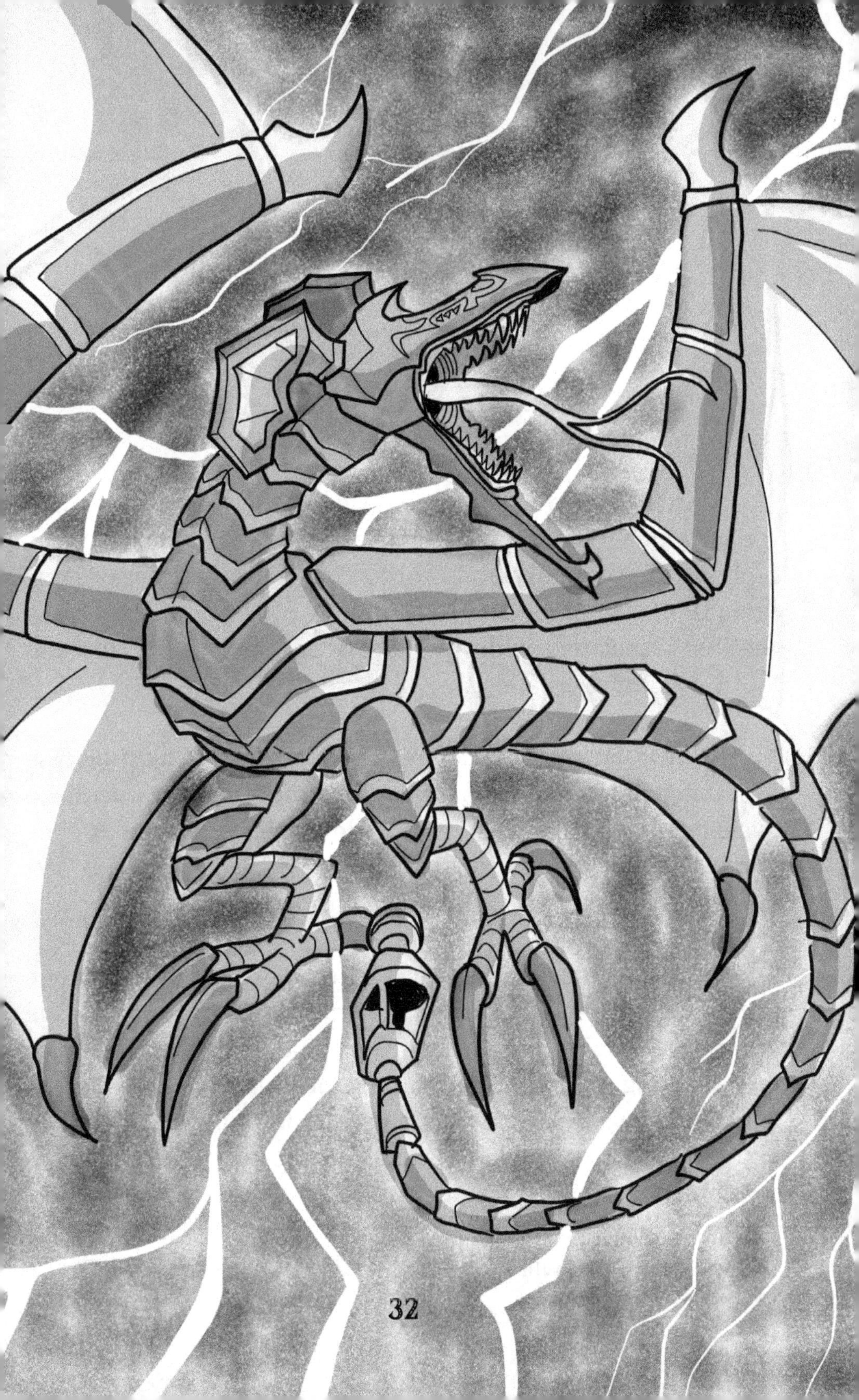

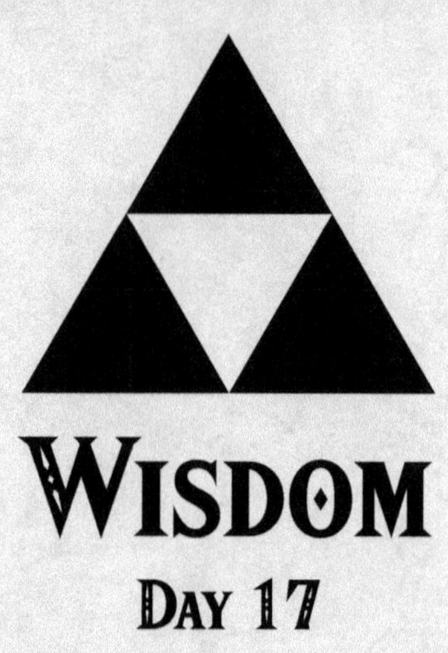

WISDOM
DAY 17

According to legend passed down by the Royal Family, the individual Triforce pieces may at times seek out those who embody their primary traits and choose them as their wielder. Princess Zelda possesses the Triforce of Wisdom, the piece that is associated with the Goddess Nayru, who brought law & order into creation.

The Triforce of Wisdom is a difficult one to showcase in a tangible way. She is seen on more than one occasion wielding magic, but that is not an ability exclusive to her. Though her darkness-sealing abilities has its roots in her divine bloodline, being a descendant of the Goddess Hylia.

The Triforce of Power is easy to depict through Ganondorf's strength and might. Even the Triforce of Courage is accurately portrayed through Link, who bravely wanders the land, battling monsters, and putting life & limb to save Hyrule. Zelda, meanwhile, isn't sitting on a throne dispensing words of wisdom like King Solomon of old. So, what does Zelda's wisdom look like in-game?

The answer will likely be made clear in *Echoes of Wisdom*.

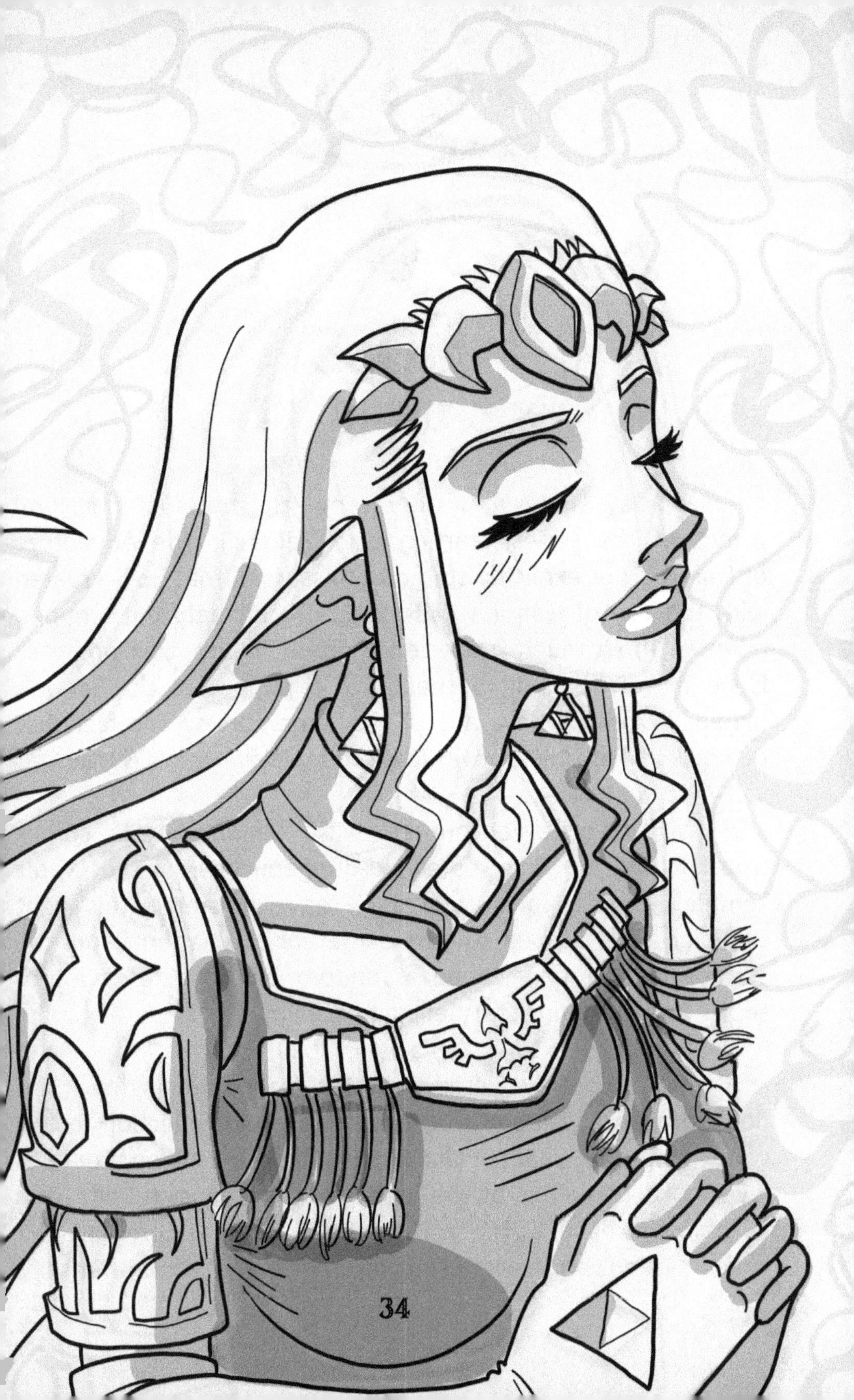

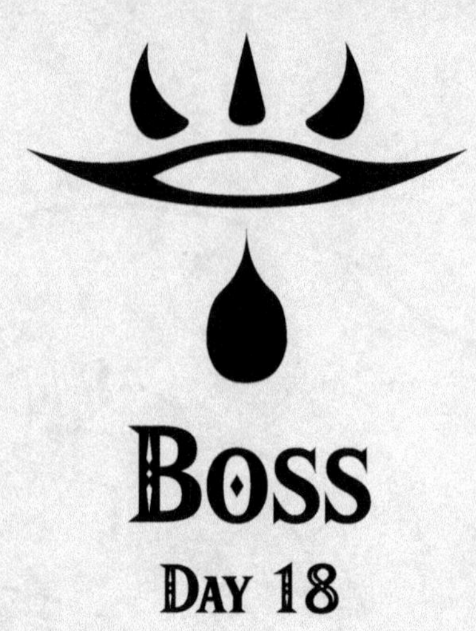

Boss

Day 18

Shadow Link is a mystery to me. He shows up in several games of the series, starting with *Zelda II: The Adventure of Link*. It's not explicitly stated but assumed that he is created with the use of Ganon's evil magic. I can't help but wonder, however, how much free agency does Shadow Link possess? Is he merely a shell of the hero, a puppet to do Ganon's bidding? Does he have any of Link's memories? The fact that he knows all of Link's moves leads me to believe this is true.

My favorite encounter with Shadow Link comes from *Ocarina of Time*, as a mid-dungeon boss in the Water Temple. Original fans, such as I, have bolstered this fight to epic levels in our collective memory. What may on the surface level appear to be a random battle, hides a lot of subtle and intriguing storytelling possibilities.

The arena is covered in water, transforming the entire floor into an aquatic mirror. Does the overt reflection in the water symbolize Shadow Link is connected to Link on a deeper level? Like two sides of the same coin, perhaps the altruistic hero might have some tendencies that he suppresses and keeps hidden, an ever-present internal battle within himself?

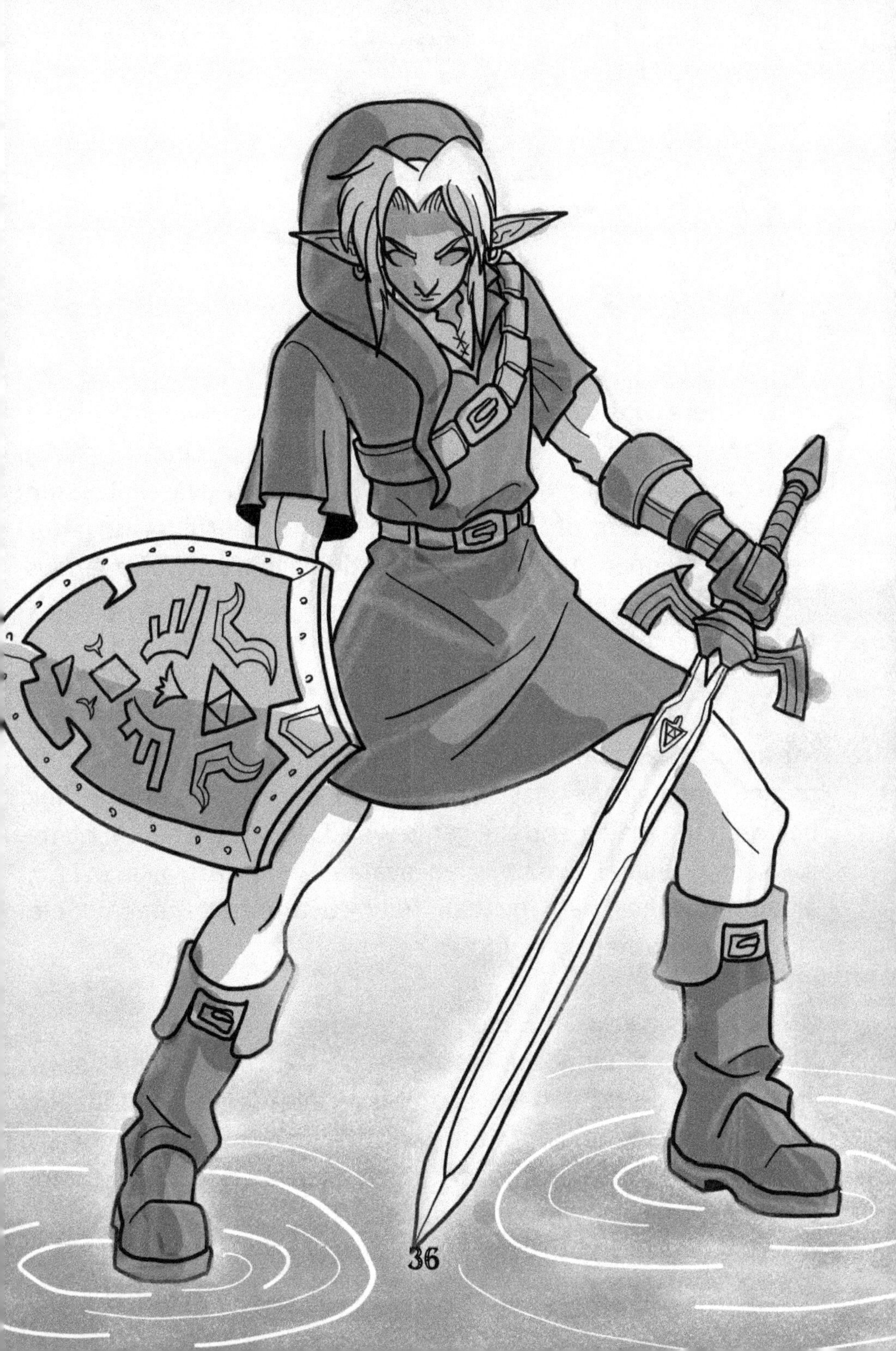

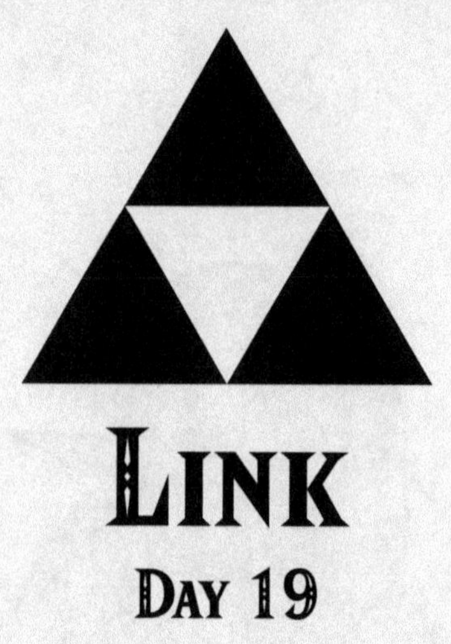

LINK

DAY 19

There was no question which character I would choose to draw on this day. Even so, I had a catalog of Links to select from, for which to depict in epic fashion. It was a toss-up between the Hero of Time and the Hero of the Wilds, the latter being the winner in this case. I already have plenty of previous artwork from *Ocarina of Time* and a new generation of gamers will likely have a stronger connection to this iteration of Link.

The creator of the Legend of Zelda series, Shigeru Miyamoto, has said from the very beginning that Link was aptly named because he was supposed to be a metaphorical link between the player and the game world. Today, we have a name for such a digital dynamic, an avatar. Link is a player avatar, albeit not one that you can fully customize as one would expect from other types of games.

To his credit, however, most games in the series allowed the player to rename the hero to whatever they wished. In my childhood, I do recall having named my file "James" and feeling such a strong immersion in the narrative. To this day, I feel uneasy committing crimes in games with my name attached to them, even though it's fiction. However, breaking pots is the exception.

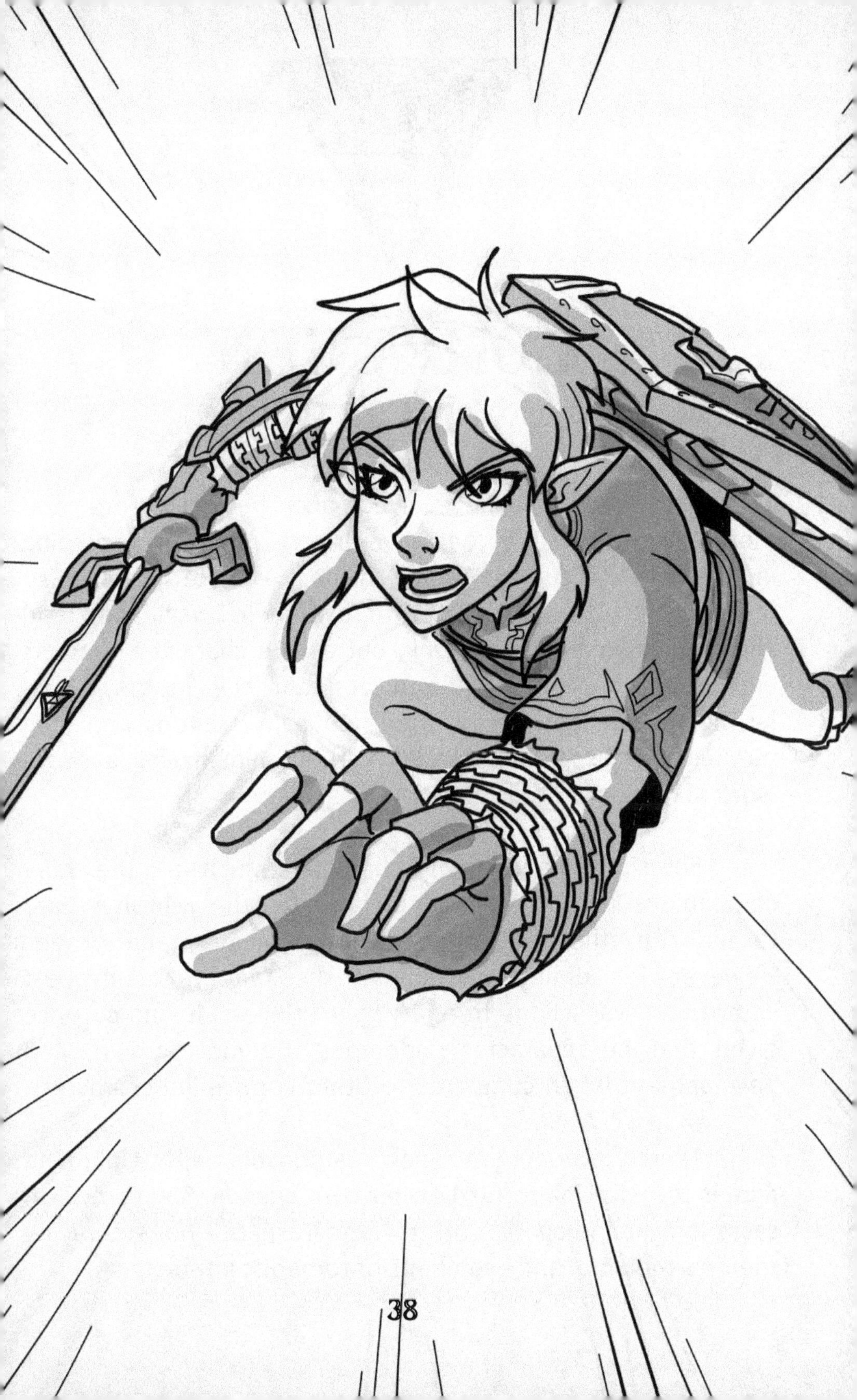

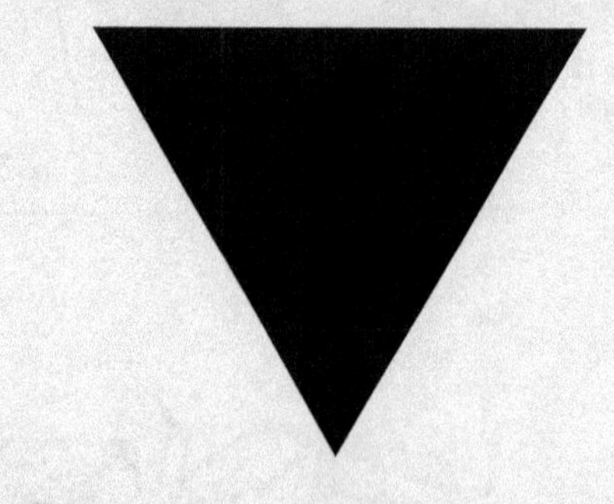

COMPANION
DAY 20

As videos games evolved and became more and more cinematic and narrative-driven, it was becoming increasingly difficult to justify having a mute protagonist. It's one thing for the player to use their imagination and give their own "voice" to Link, but as the character interacts with the world and NPCs throughout the journey, it is jarring to constantly read one-sided conversations and long moments of exposition to Link without him having a single word of response other than "hyah" and "hmm".

Enter the companion characters such as the fairy companions (Navi, Tatl, and Ciela), Alzo the Minish wizard turned cap, the King of Red Lions sailboat, and others. However, it's unanimous among the fans that the best companion was Midna from *Twilight Princess*. It's no surprise given that her character undergoes the most growth and development when compared to other companion characters.

There is nuance to her relationship with Link. She agrees to help Link to further her own agenda. She comes off sassy and unapologetic but grows to respect Link, embracing their partnership, and even hints of romantic interest.

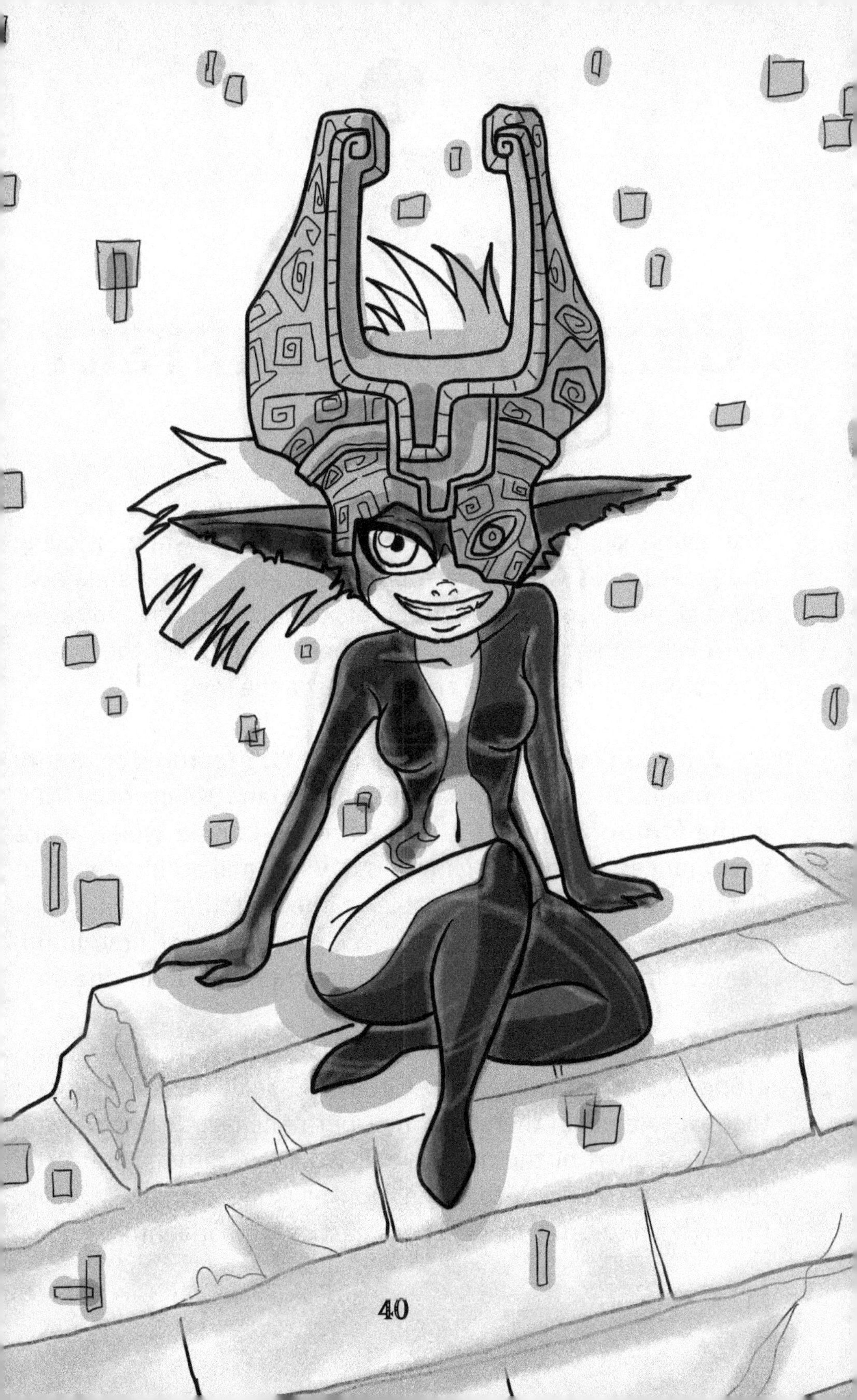

GRAVEYARD/CEMETERY
DAY 21

Graveyards have been a part of the series since the very first game on the Nintendo Entertainment System. Moving the gravestones would make ghosts appear. It's a well-known video game mechanic to hide secrets behind waterfalls, in caves, and even under graves. It's risky because moving the wrong gravestone will result in a enemy ghost appearing.

It wasn't until *Ocarina of Time* that the featured cemetery was finally given an official designated and reoccurring NPC in the form of Dampé the grave-keeper. Dampé would make appearances in several games but what makes his debut in *Ocarina of Time* so memorable is the fact that in the later half of the game, which takes place after a 7-year time jump, Dampé himself becomes a ghost; Thankfully a friendly one.

When taking a step back and looking at other Nintendo properties, it's startling to see that the Zelda series is among the few to contain themes of non-permanence, death, and the afterlife as part of the narrative. It would be rather odd to see the likes of Mario, Kirby, and Donkey Kong casually strolling through a dedicated cemetery as part of their adventures.

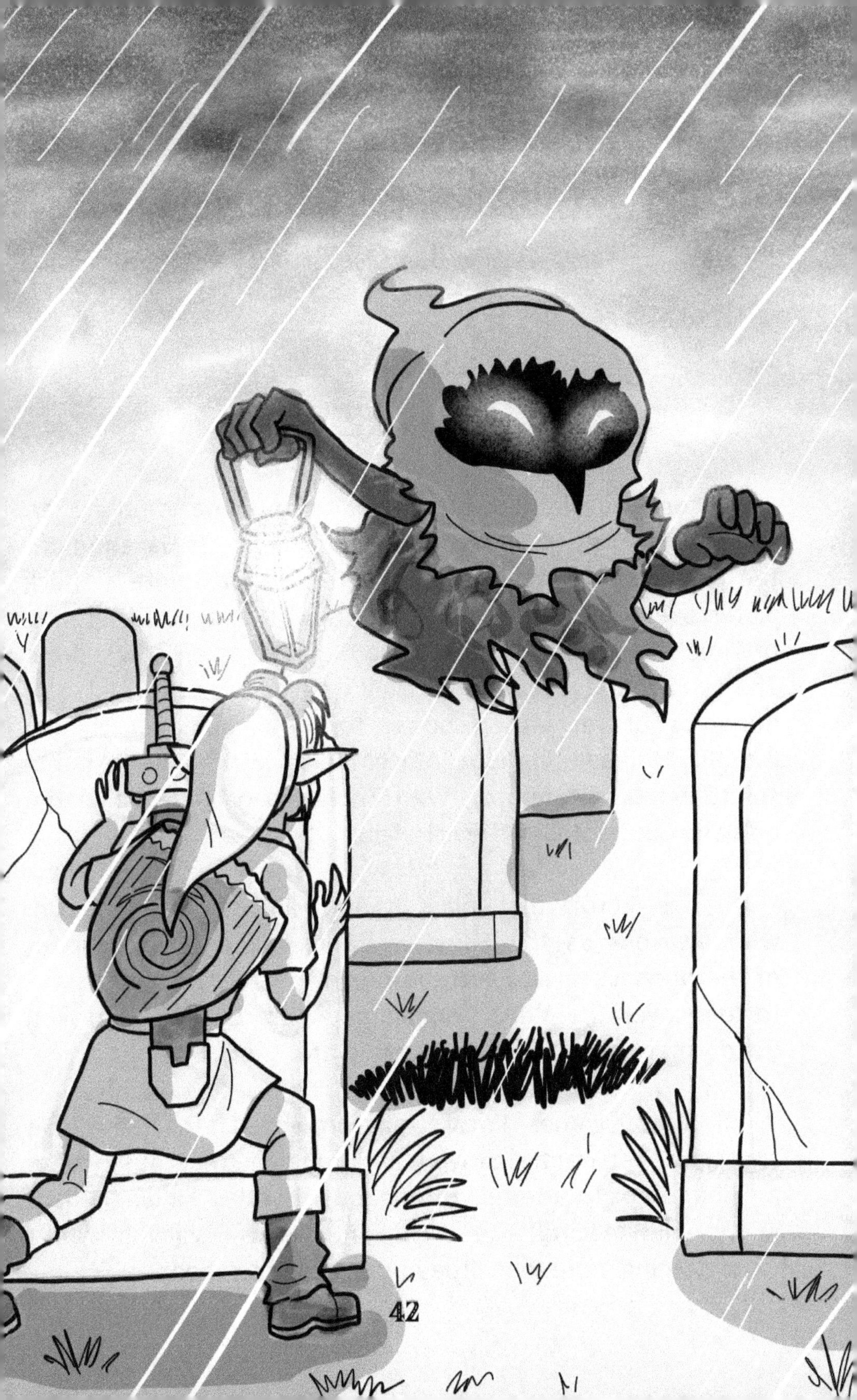

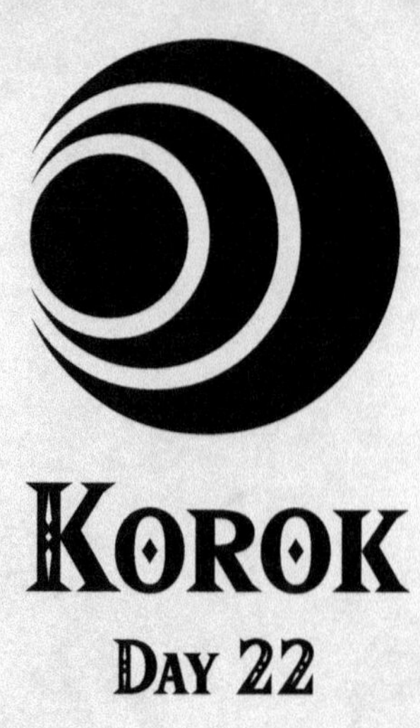

KOROK

DAY 22

Koroks make their first appearance in *The Wind Waker*, as the cute forest dwellers that live in the Forest Haven under the protection of the Great Deku Tree. It was quite a shock to discover they were actually one and the same of *Ocarina of Time*'s Kokiri tribe, which were depicted as elvish children. The explanation given is that they evolved over the course of hundreds of years in response to the flooding of Hyrule. Although human in appearance, Kokiri were always forest spirits first and foremost, with The Hero of Time being the odd one out because he was Hylian.

This Korok that plays the violin is named Makar, who awakens as the Sage of Wind and is a descendant of the previous sage, Fado the Kokiri. His role in the game is to look over the Wind Temple and help Link to reawaken the dormant power of the Master Sword.

In later games, Koroks take on less of a narrative role and have apparently thrived and multiplied because there are hundreds scattered throughout Hyrule. Finding them in the wild rewards Link with Korok seeds, which turn out to be nothing more than little nuggets of Korok poop.

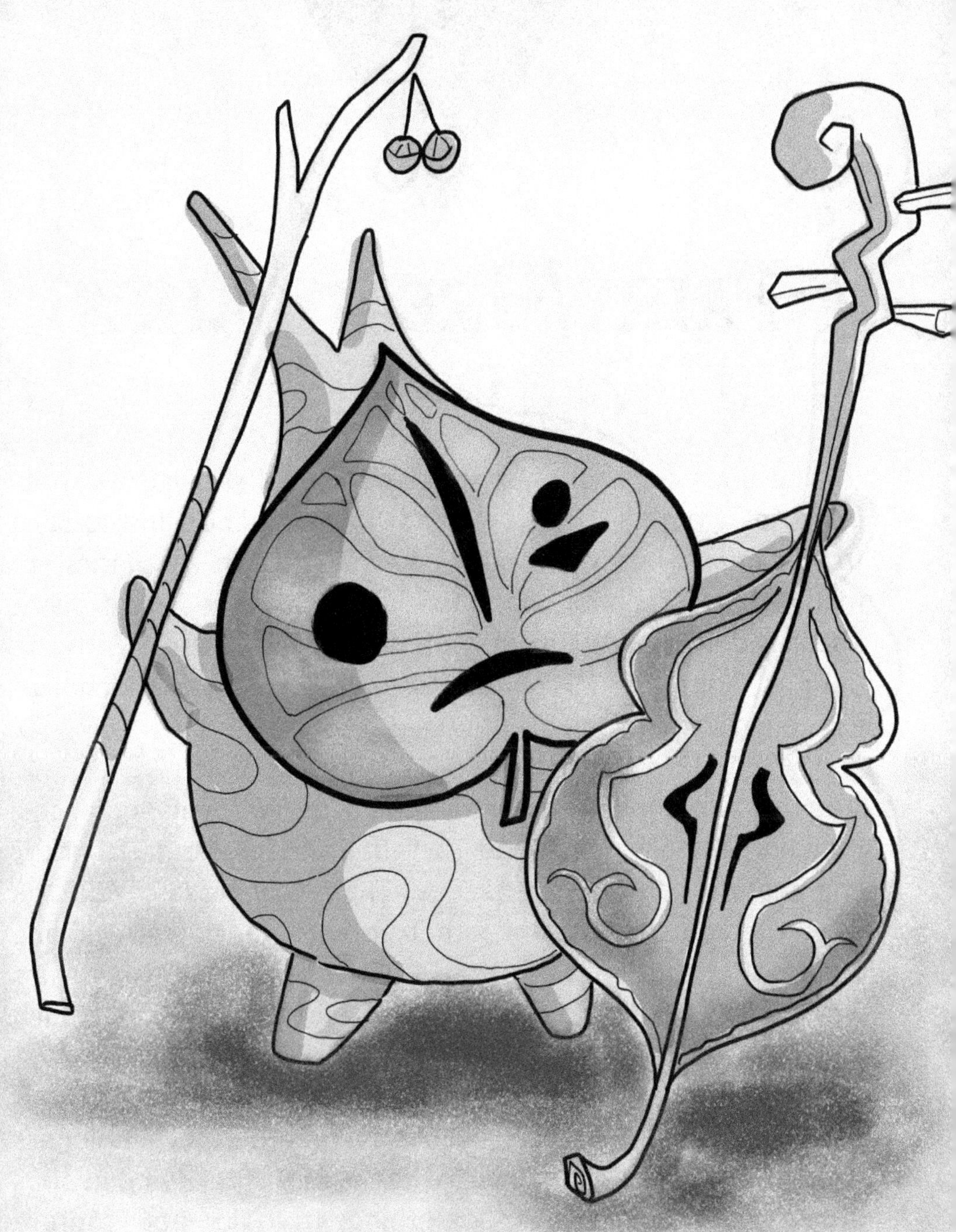

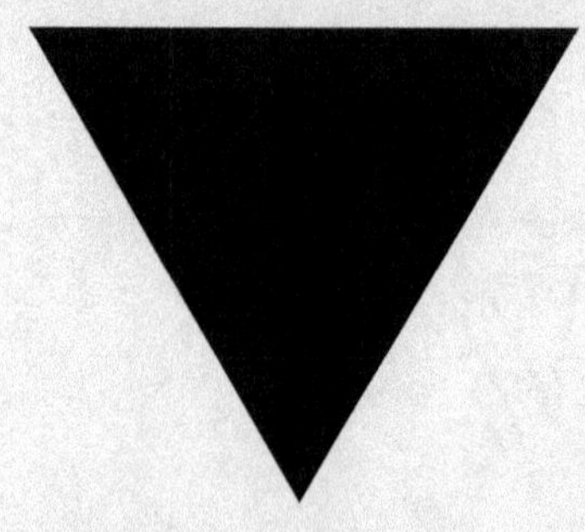

Fairy/Great Fairy
Day 23

    Fairies come in all shapes and sizes. I showed a variety of fairies from the Day 2 prompt. The variation in art style from game to game translates to a change in aesthetics of many creatures and characters, including the Great Fairy. There is quite a range from wholesome, fully robed & intricate designs from the 2D games to more scantily clad choices as seen in some of the 3D titles.

    In Nintendo's effort to appeal to Western audiences, they purposefully developed *Twilight Princess* as a dark, gritty, and mature game in the series. Their goal was to ride the wave of success seen from other popular franchises including *The Lord of the Rings* and *Harry Potter*. Perhaps this explains why this unique version of the Great Fairy is portrayed in such a revealing fashion.

    What may be at first glance risqué, there is simpleness to her design, hearkening to something more indigenous rather than suggestive. Something I could not capture with justice in my drawing is the majestic rendering of her multiple pairs of colorful ethereal wings. Meeting her in-game is quite difficult to achieve so the reward to the player is great.

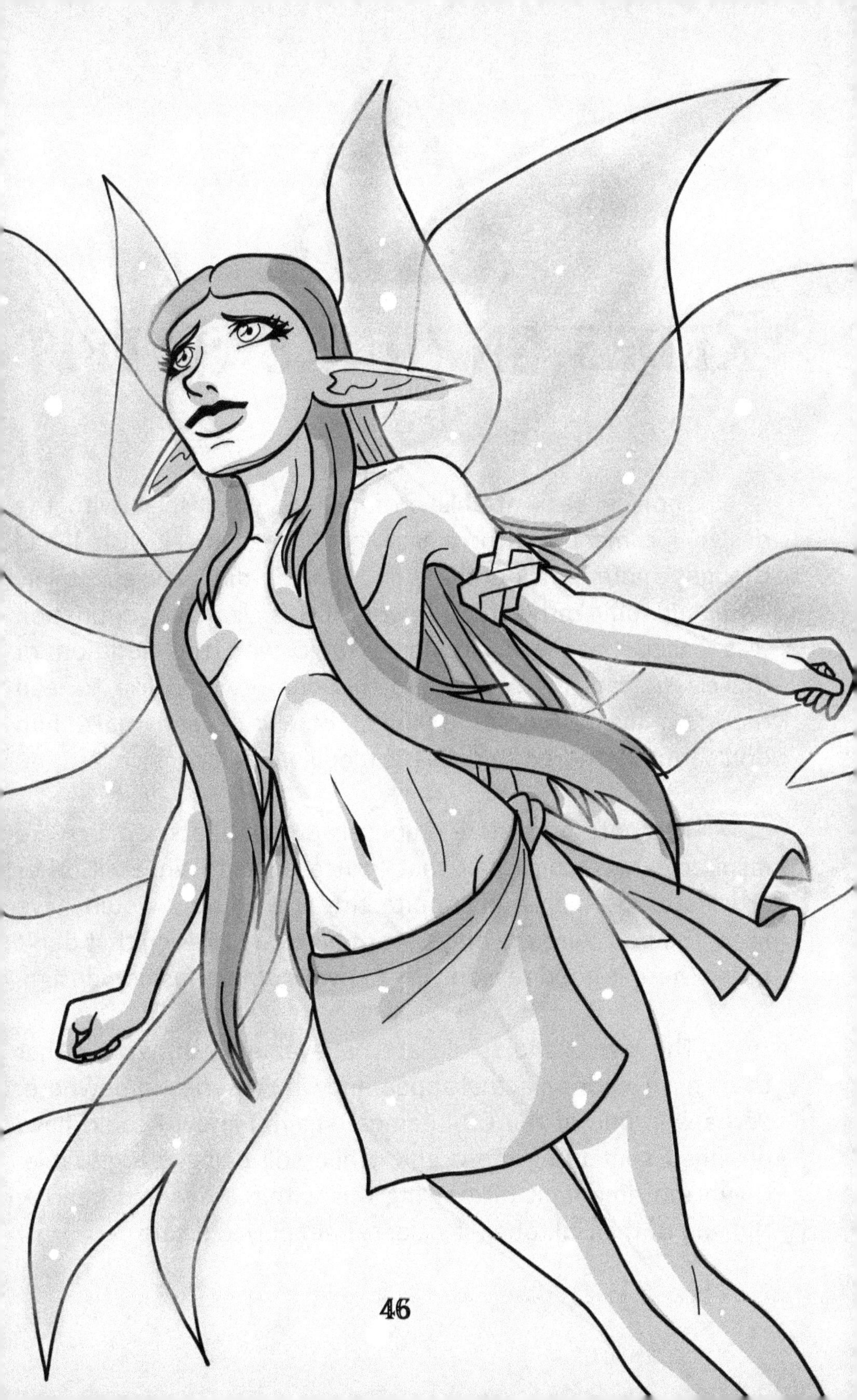

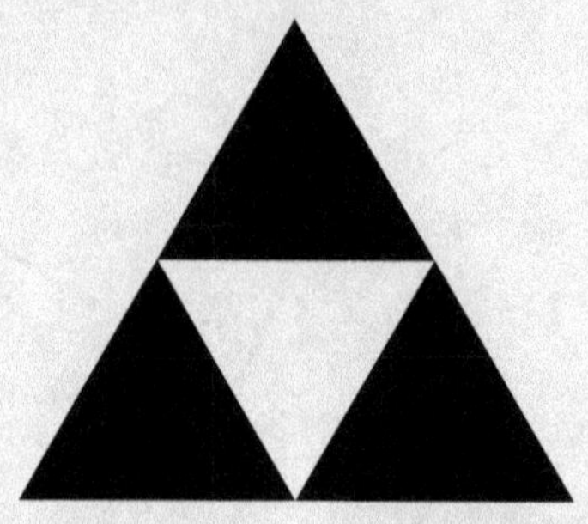

REDESIGN LINK'S OUTFIT
DAY 24

Looking back at this prompt, I'm unsatisfied with the design I came up with, which lacks creativity. I wish I had thought more outside the box. What I did was effectively remix his tunic rather than rework it. It's clear the foundation was based on the Champion's Tunic with the addition of the classic cap. If I could redo this one, I would like to lean more on his history as a knight of Hyrule and make him don a more armored suit, classic medieval style.

This pose puts more emphasis on the boots, which were inspired by a tactical pair that I once owned. While all other articles of clothing aren't quite the change-up I would have liked, the boots are the only part of his overall design that don't fit in. There is good reason that I never got into fashion design.

The sword and shield are believable as something that could have made an actual appearance in the series somewhere. Perhaps in one of the CD-i games. Again, I know I could have designed something more epic while still being recognizable. Given the time limit of drawing this within a day and nearing the end of the Linktober, it's clear that I played it safe.

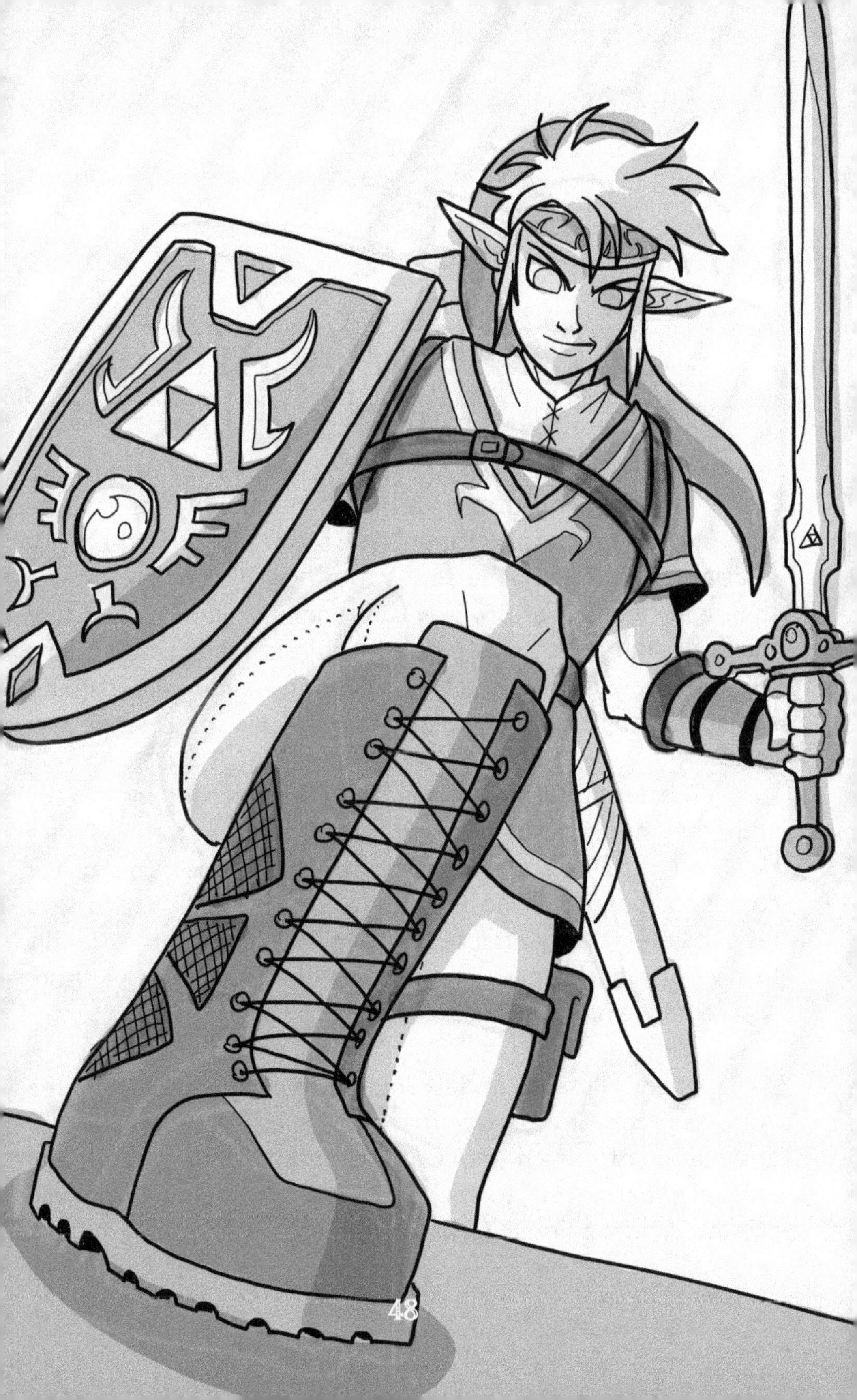

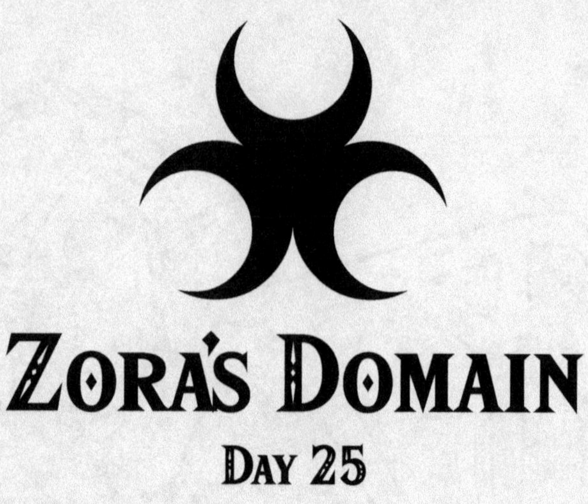

Zora's Domain
Day 25

Although *Twilight Princess* isn't necessarily my favorite game in the series, I think I appreciate the art direction the most. *Ocarina of Time* took the series to a new dimension, making the jump from 2D to 3D, it wasn't until *Twilight Princess* that the scale and depth was properly realized for both the game world as well as its characters. All towns, landmark locations, and supporting cast of characters increased in size & scope.

The narrative surrounding Zora's Domain contains tragedy with the murder of Queen Rutela, leaving her son, Prince Ralis, an orphan and successor to the throne. The player comes to the aid of The Prince more than once, first to save his life after being attacked & left for dead, and secondly to give him back hope & purpose after experiencing closure & acceptance of his mother's passing.

Queen Rutela, a descendant of the Sage of Water, Princess Ruto from *Ocarina of Time*, was wonderfully designed with much more ornamentation, fin decor, and uniquely warm red tones made her stand out from the previously cool-colored Zora from the past.

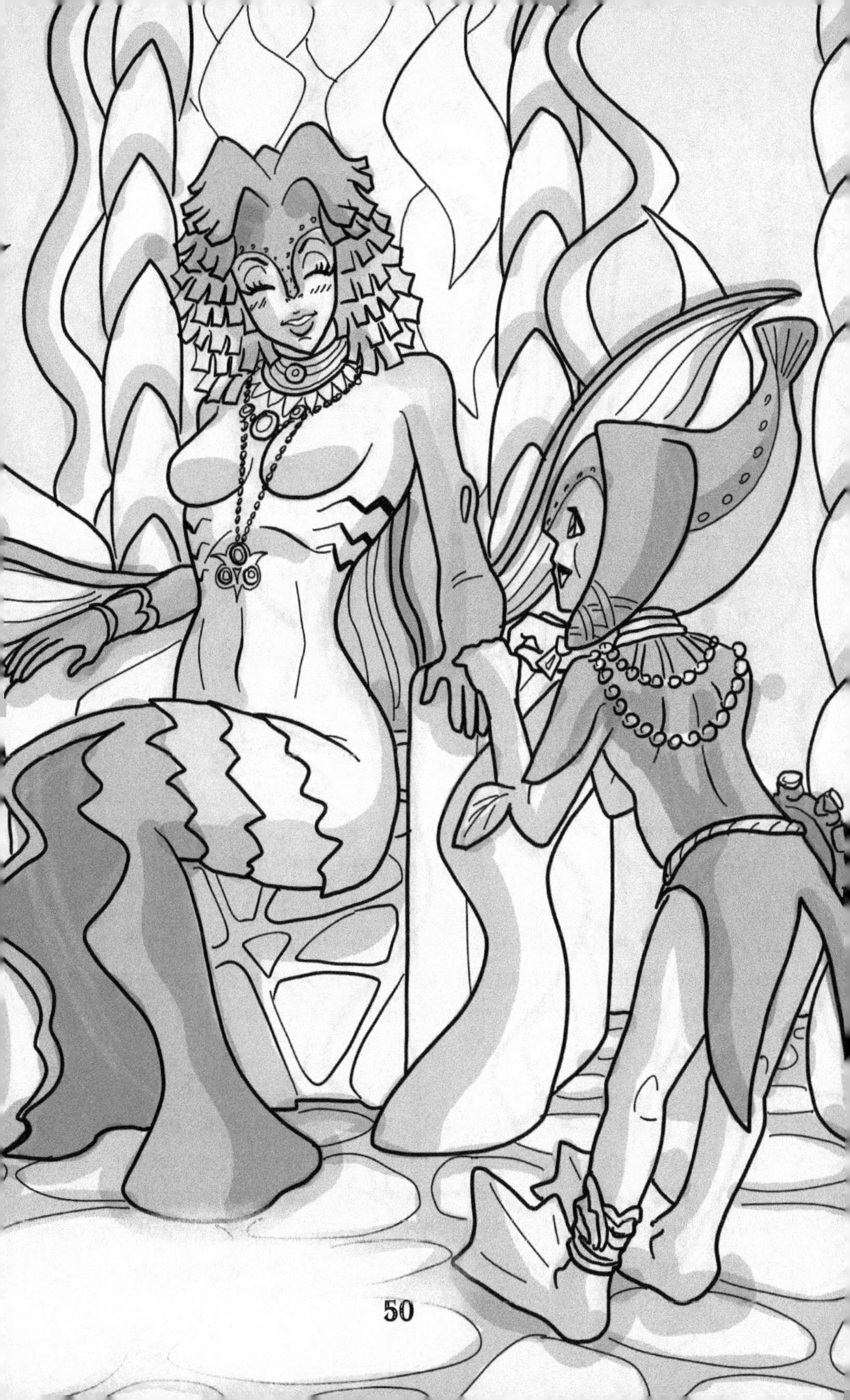

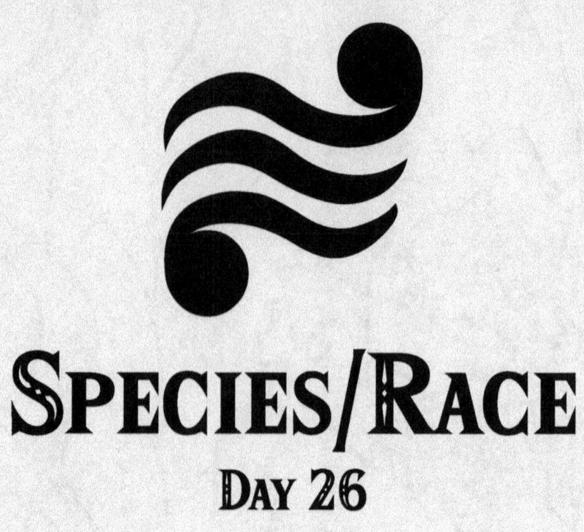

Species/Race
Day 26

As I approached near the end of Linktober, I was happy to use this opportunity to draw some of the unique characters for my first time. The Zelda series is rich with heroes and villains of various species, races, and forms. The variety keeps me on my toes because different types of creatures have unique anatomies and looks. This is challenging as an artist but also healthy as it requires illustrating consciously and stepping out of my comfort zone.

I chose to illustrate Medli, the Sage of Earth, from *The Wind Waker*. She is a member of the Rito Tribe, which evolved from the Zora, similar to the Kokiri transition into Korok. At first glance, the Rito appear to look like Hylians with the exception of a bird beak instead of a nose. When they come of age, they develop a full set of wings which sprout from their arms on demand.

The Rito make their first appearance in this game, but their species would continue to change as later games would depict them fully avian, no longer having any resemblance to Hylians; even less so the Zora. The Rito become a tribe of fully realized bird-people, even the young can fly before maturation.

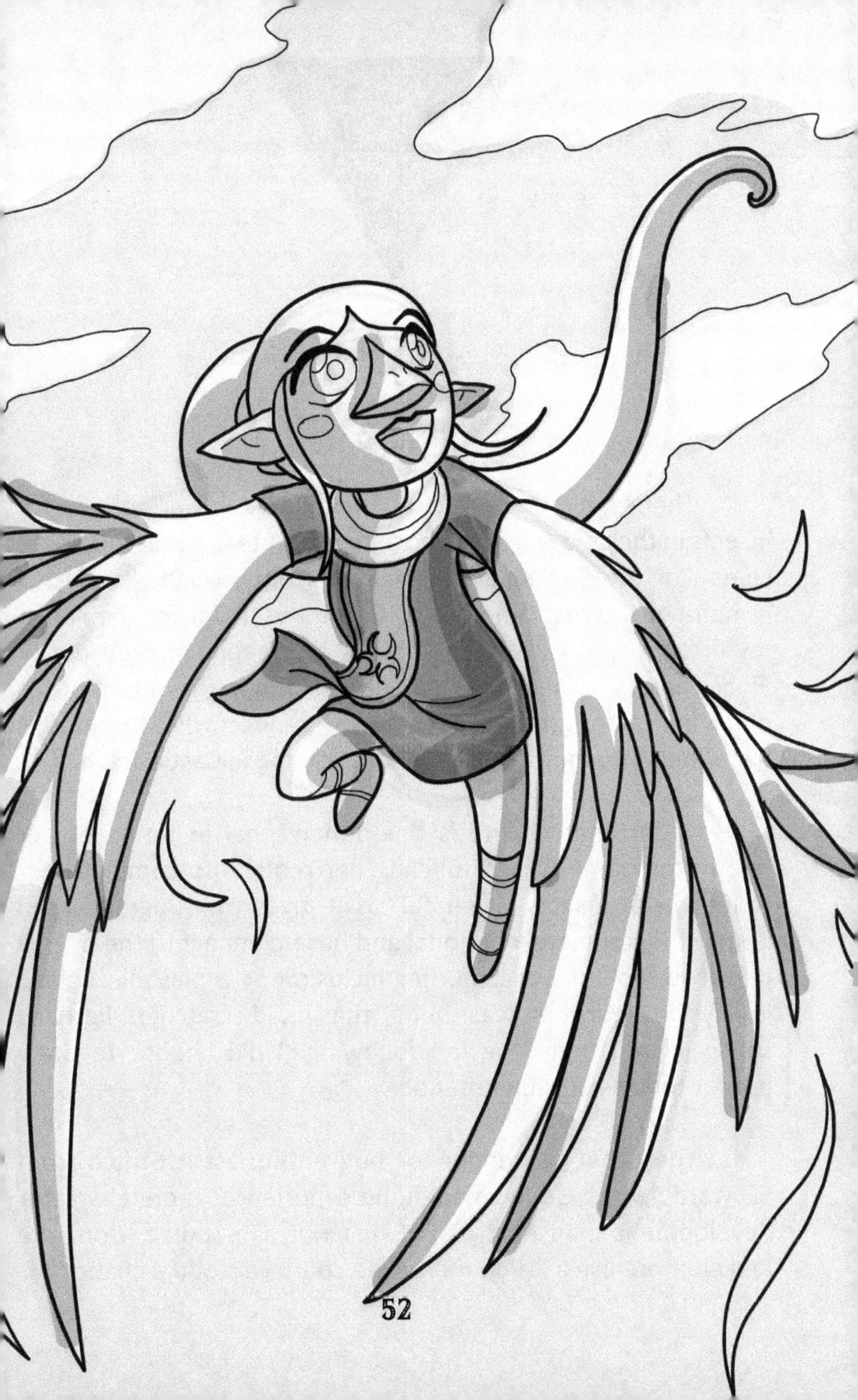

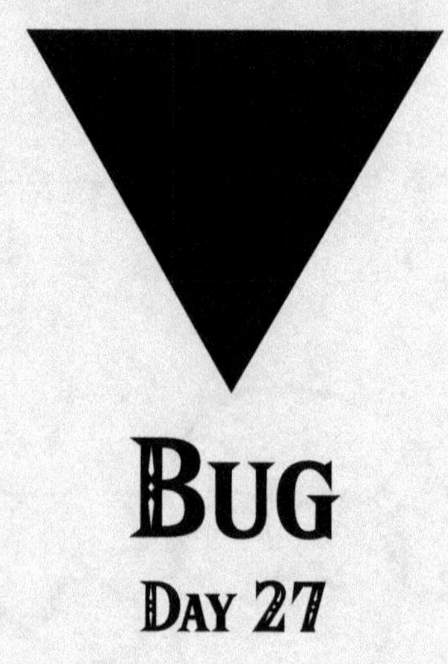

BUG
DAY 27

There have been several characters with an affinity for insects in the Zelda series. I chose to illustrate the self-appointed Queen of the Bug Kingdom, Agatha from *Twilight Princess*. I remember the first time seeing her in the trailer for the game, my first thought was "she looks like a someone straight out of *Final Fantasy*". There was something about the attention to detail in her design, especially for a side-quest NPC, that makes her stand out among other Hylians residing in Castle Town.

Unfortunately, she is one-dimensional in terms of her role in the game. While fulfilling her request to complete her collection of insects is helpful, as it gives Link upgrades and items, it is completely optional and has no impact to the overall narrative. For that reason, her inclusion as a playable fighter in *Hyrule Warriors* was quite the head-scratcher. Perhaps she garnered quite the fan following. I did choose to draw her for today's prompt, after all.

The other contender for bug enthusiast is Stritch from *Skyward Sword*. Oddly enough, he experiences more character development than Agatha, but he's not as popular. If only he looked more like a K-Pop model, he could've stood a chance.

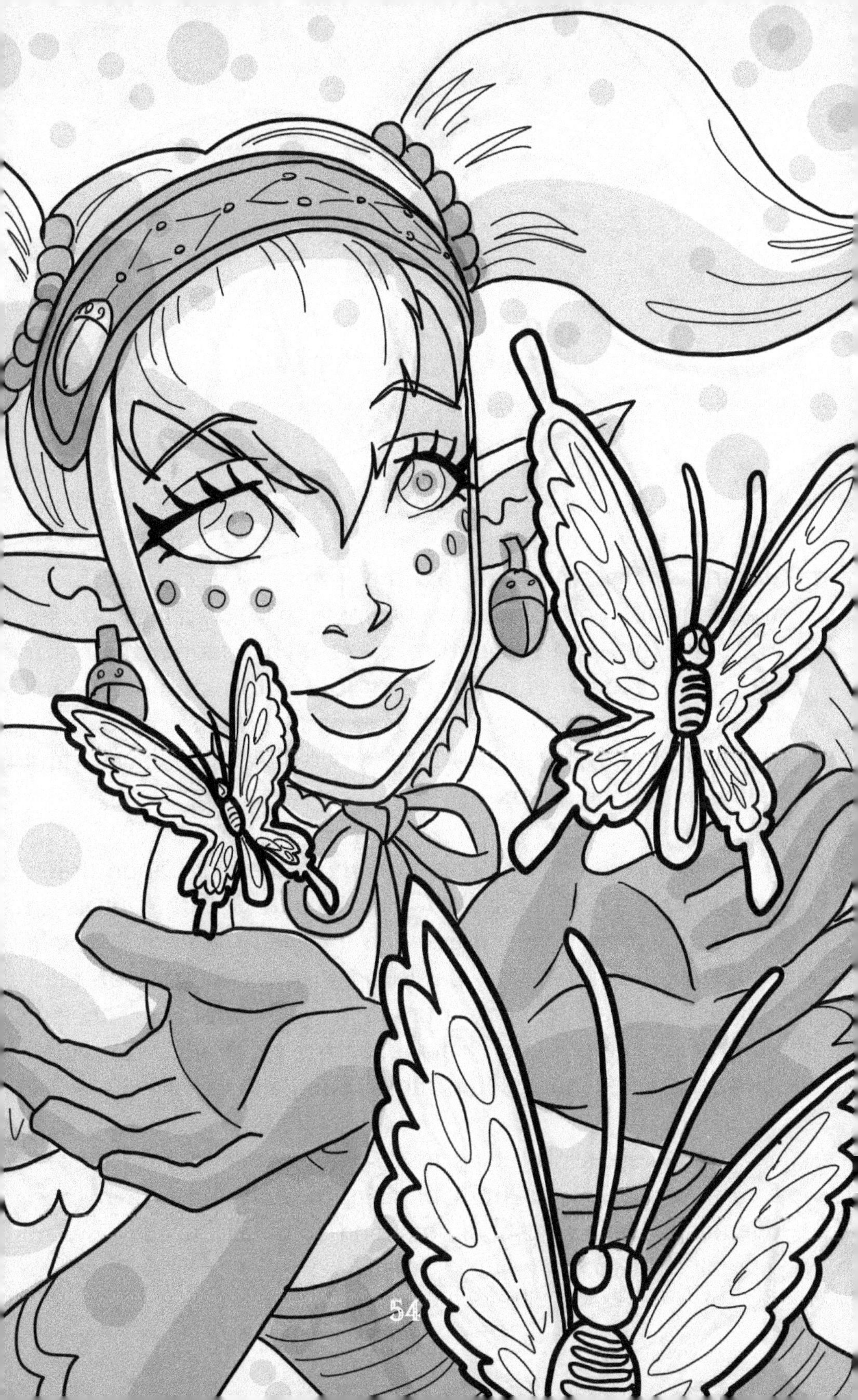

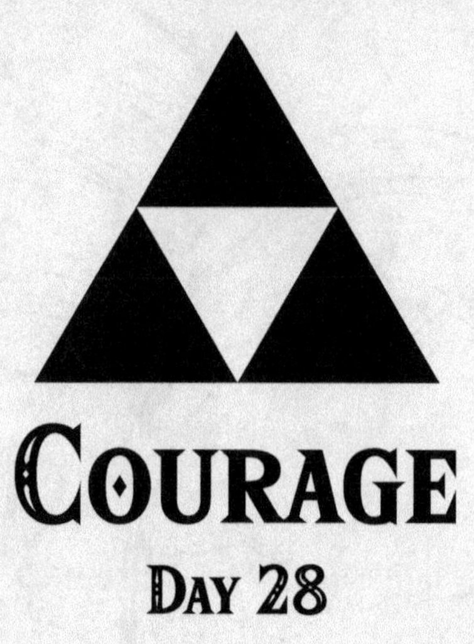

COURAGE
DAY 28

I've already addressed the other two parts of the Triforce, Power and Wisdom. The component of Courage is unsurprisingly embodied by the protagonist, Link. It's no wonder why. The game usually begins with Link waking from bed and being thrust into adventure as a result of a sudden trauma or loss. The character of Link goes on "The Hero's Journey": Starting out as a humble youth and developing into the chosen hero through prowess in combat, using wits at puzzle-solving, and selflessly serving others.

The visual of Link standing up to the evil Ganon draws parallels to the biblical tale of David and Goliath. Link is an elvish boy of small stature who takes up sword & shield and runs headfirst into battle against the largest of foes, including dragons, rock monsters, giant spiders, ancient automatons, and demon kings. I can't think of any other video game character that exhibits more courage than Link.

I believe Link serves as a great role model for players to look up to. Aside from breaking & entering NPC homes, unapologetically smashing pots, and stabbing Cuccos, I swear he really is hero material!

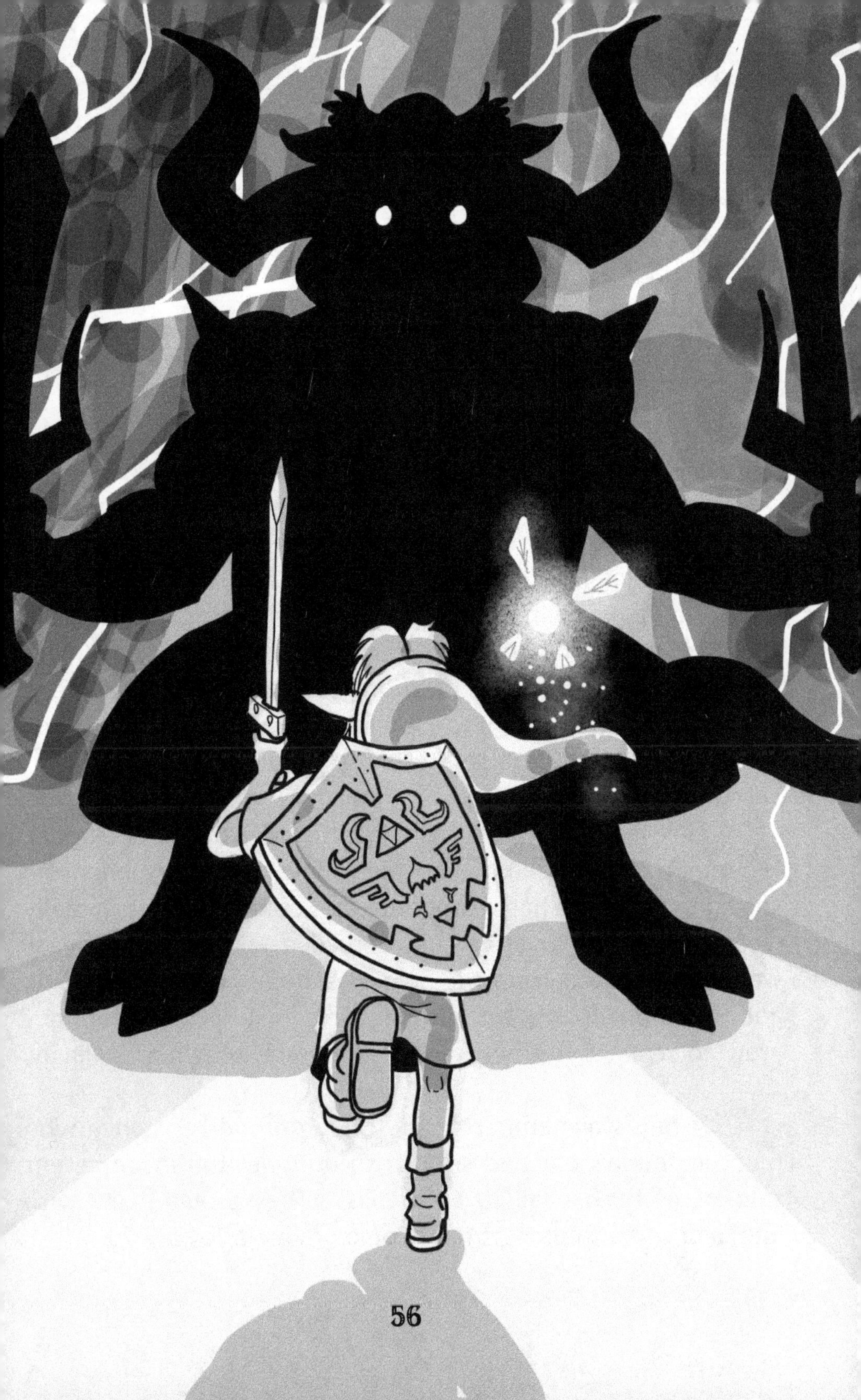

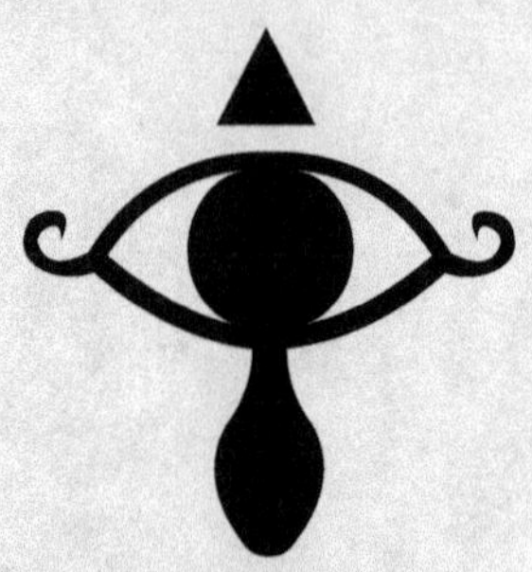

NPC Non-Player Character

Day 29

Casual Zelda players might not immediately recognize this character, who only made an appearance in a single game, *Twilight Princess*. Her name is Ashei. She is a part of a small band of Hylians who take a stand against evil and aid Link throughout his journey. Her father was a Hylian Knight and trained her in the art of sword combat as well as archery. I found her armor design to be intricate and interesting, which is why I chose her for today's prompt.

Link first encounters Ashei at the foot of the Snowpeak Mountains. She was in the middle of investigating rumors of a snow monster who has an appetite for Reekfish. Ashei is initially wearing a facial covering that served as both a disguise as well as protection from the cold weather. She is rude to Link and emotionally distant during their first introduction but grew to respect the hero and collaborate with him willingly.

Ashei is a member of the underground resistance who meet in Telma's bar and set out to do what the incompetent soldiers of Hyrule fail to accomplish. They provide Link with intel and serve to protect the people of Castle Town.

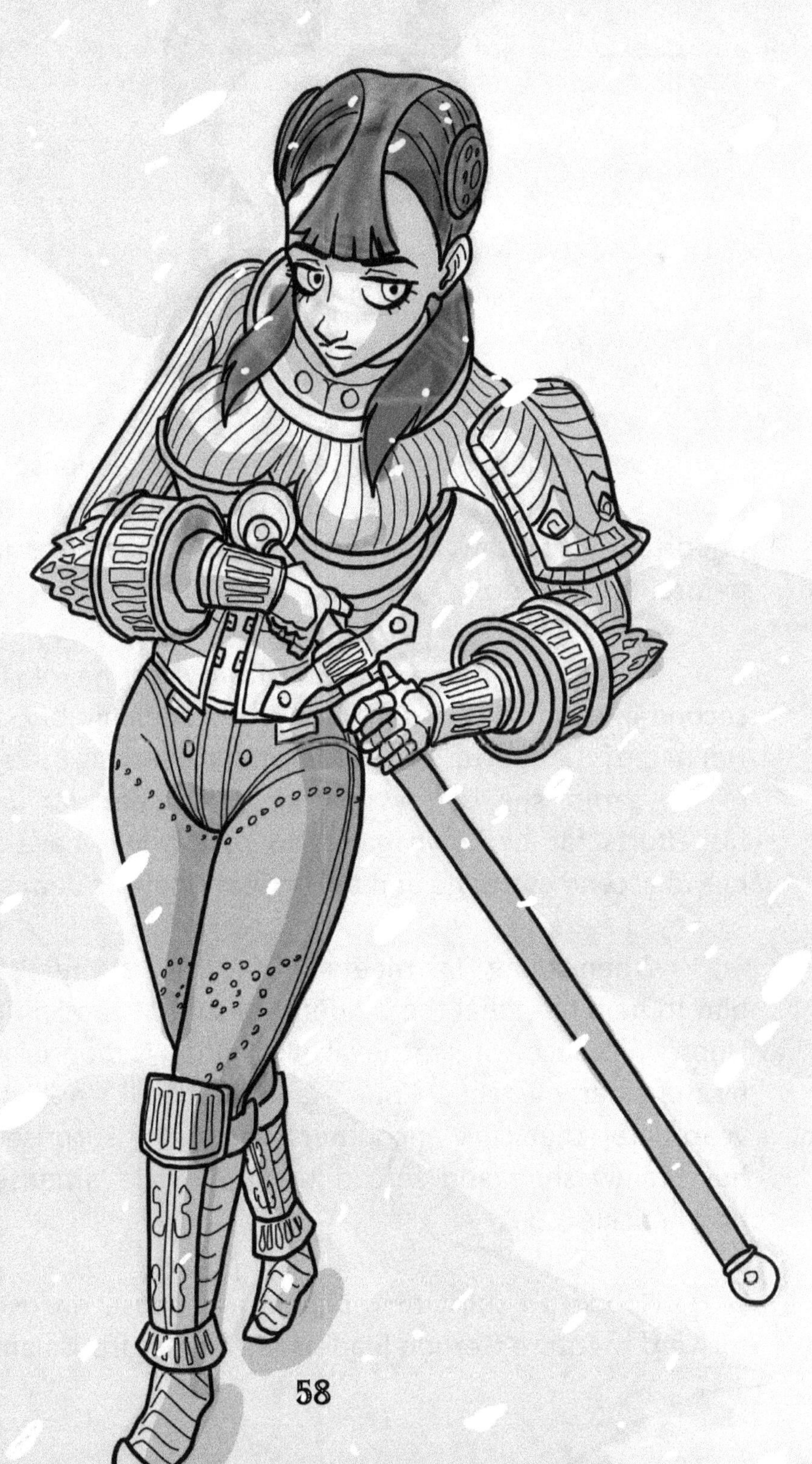

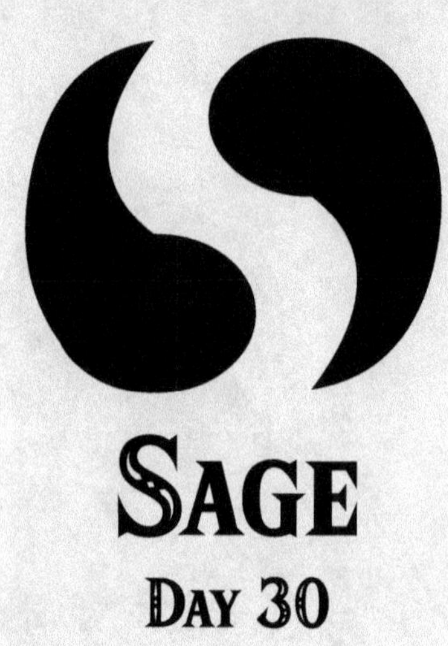

SAGE
DAY 30

I've already drawn a few sages in response to other prompts, but I wanted to choose a different one as an opportunity to draw another race that I have not illustrated before, the Gerudo.

This is the Sage of Spirit from *Ocarina of Time*, the second-in-command under the direct leadership of Ganondorf. Her name is Nabooru. Even though initially serving the antagonist of the game, she betrays her king and seeks to undermine his efforts for her own gain. No one would have expected her to ascend as a sage and aid in Gannondorf's demise.

When Young Link meets her for the first time, she enlists him to help her steal the hidden treasure of the Spirit Temple. Upon Link's successful retrieval of the prize, Nabooru is captured by the elderly witches, Koume and Kotake. It's not until seven years later that Link encounters her again, surprised to find her brainwashed and forced to fight while disguised as an Iron Knuckle.

Nabooru's spirit of rebellion and sense of justice carry forward to future Gerudo leaders, including Urbosa and Riju.

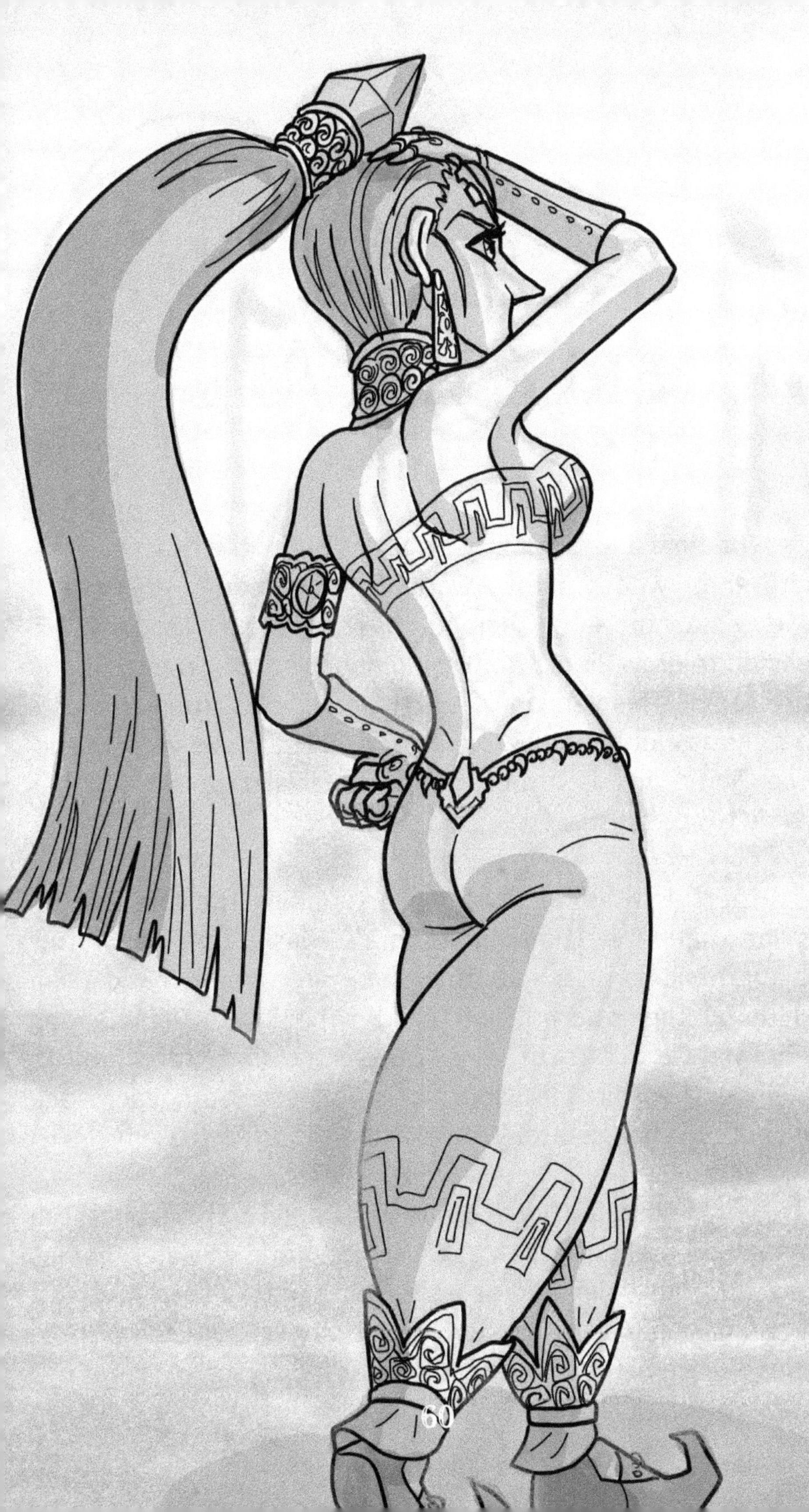

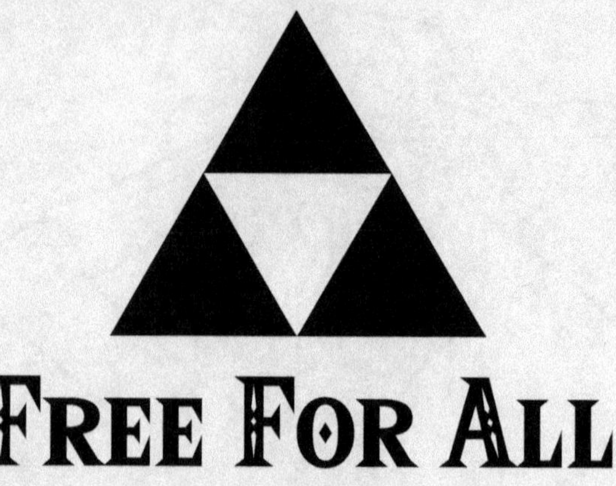

Free For All
Day 31

The final day for Linktober opens up for the artist to draw whatever or whoever they want. Funnily enough, this year I chose to draw the same character as I did during Inktober 2017. I decided to draw Fierce Deity Link, my favorite character in the entire series. This version of Link is incredibly strong, wields a two-handed double-helix longsword, and attacks with magic. Fierce Deity Link is armored, wears facial tattoos, and has glowing white eyes.

There is a lot of mystery surrounding the lore behind this incarnation of Link. In *Majora's Mask*, Link transforms into this epic form by wearing the Fierce Deity mask given to him by the lonely Moon child, who is himself wearing Majora's Mask. All of the other transformation masks contained the spirits of specific characters, from each race that Link can change into. Who exactly is this Fierce Deity?

Unfortunately, Fierce Deity Link only makes an official appearance in *Majora's Mask*. His costume in later games isn't canon but delegated as an easter egg to please the fans. It was amazing playing as the Fierce Deity Link outside of boss battles, where he was limited to play as in *Majora's Mask*.

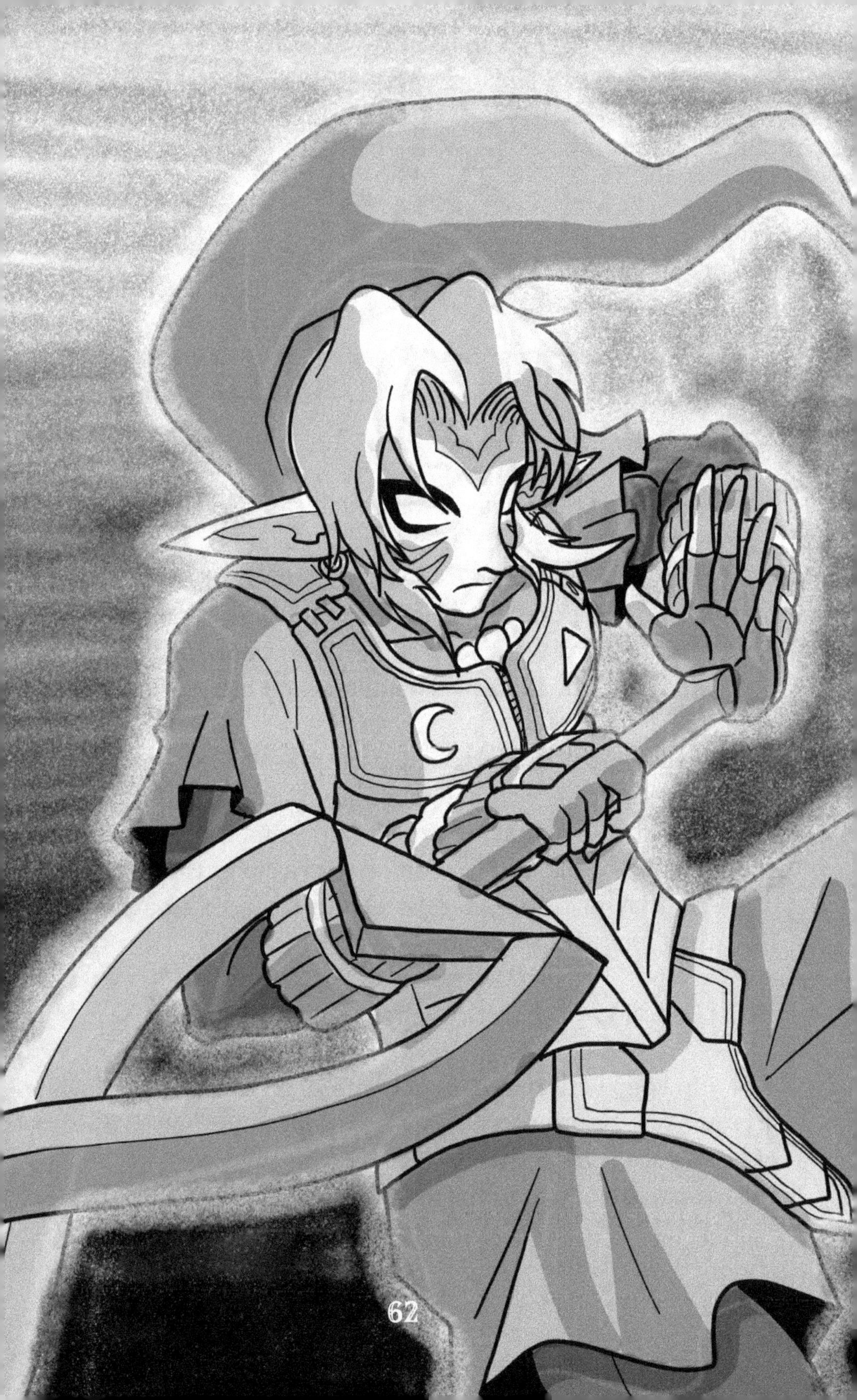

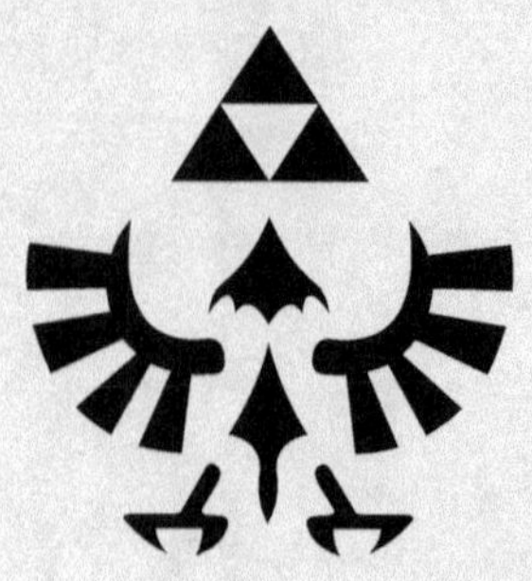

BONUS GALLERY

2019's Inktober was dedicated to the *Legend of Zelda*, but I never need to wait for the annual Linktober tradition as a valid reason to create Zelda-related content. Over the years I have sketched, doodled, inked, and fully colored dozens of illustrations, and I want to include them because this book is dedicated to all the fantastic characters and the world of Hyrule.

Following the Linktober prompts allowed me to step out of my comfort zone and illustrate many secondary heroes, villains, and NPC characters for the first time. It was a positive experience, a challenge I welcomed with a smile. However, you'll find I do play favorites as most of the fan art I create feature the titular characters of Zelda and Link.

Ganondorf doesn't get enough love. I hear ya.

To keep with the overall theme of Inktober, the following artwork will be presented in black and white line art. Many of these can be viewed in color on my website, online galleries, and popular social media accounts @jamesartville.

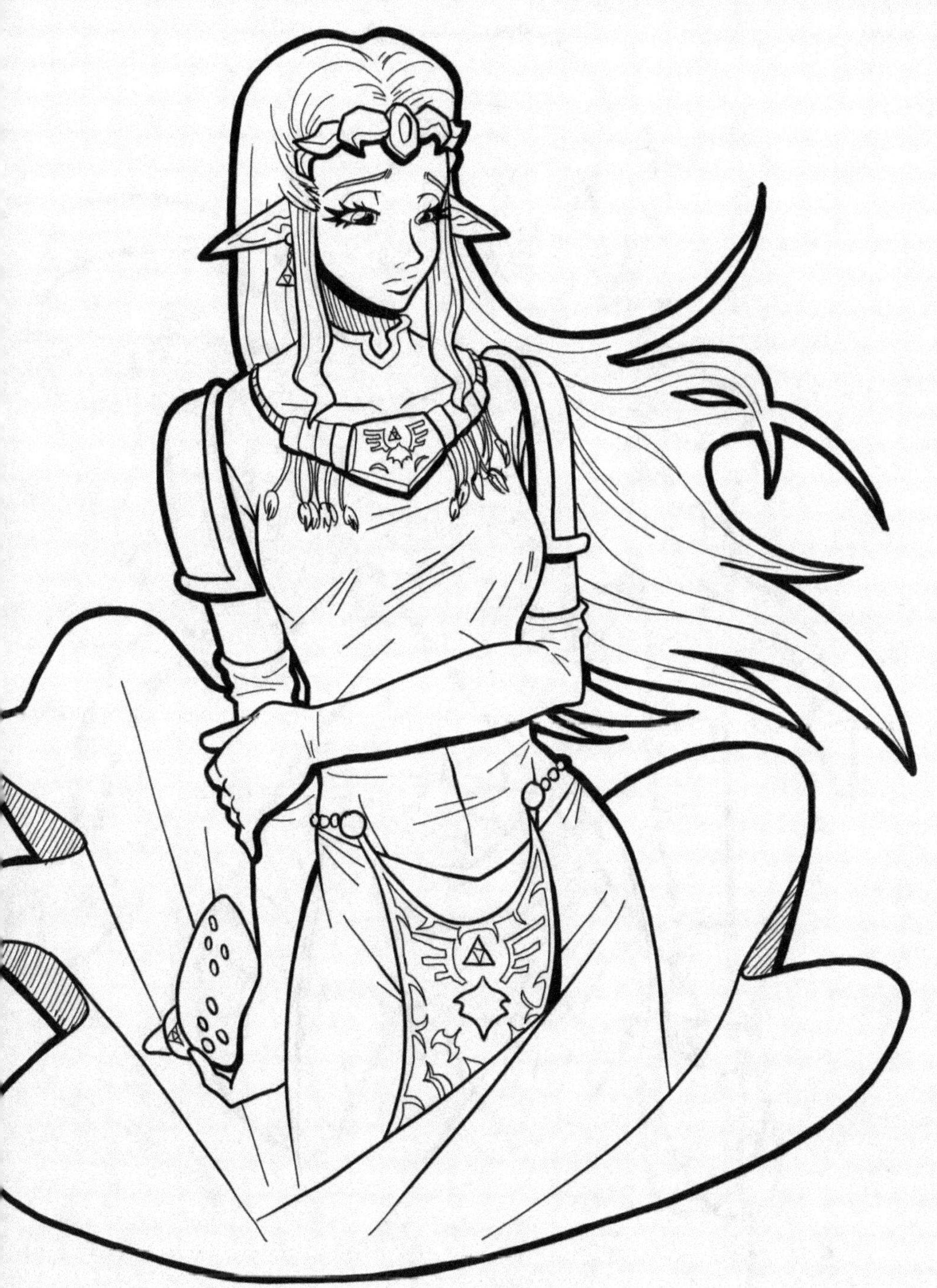

Princess Zelda from *Ocarina of Time*

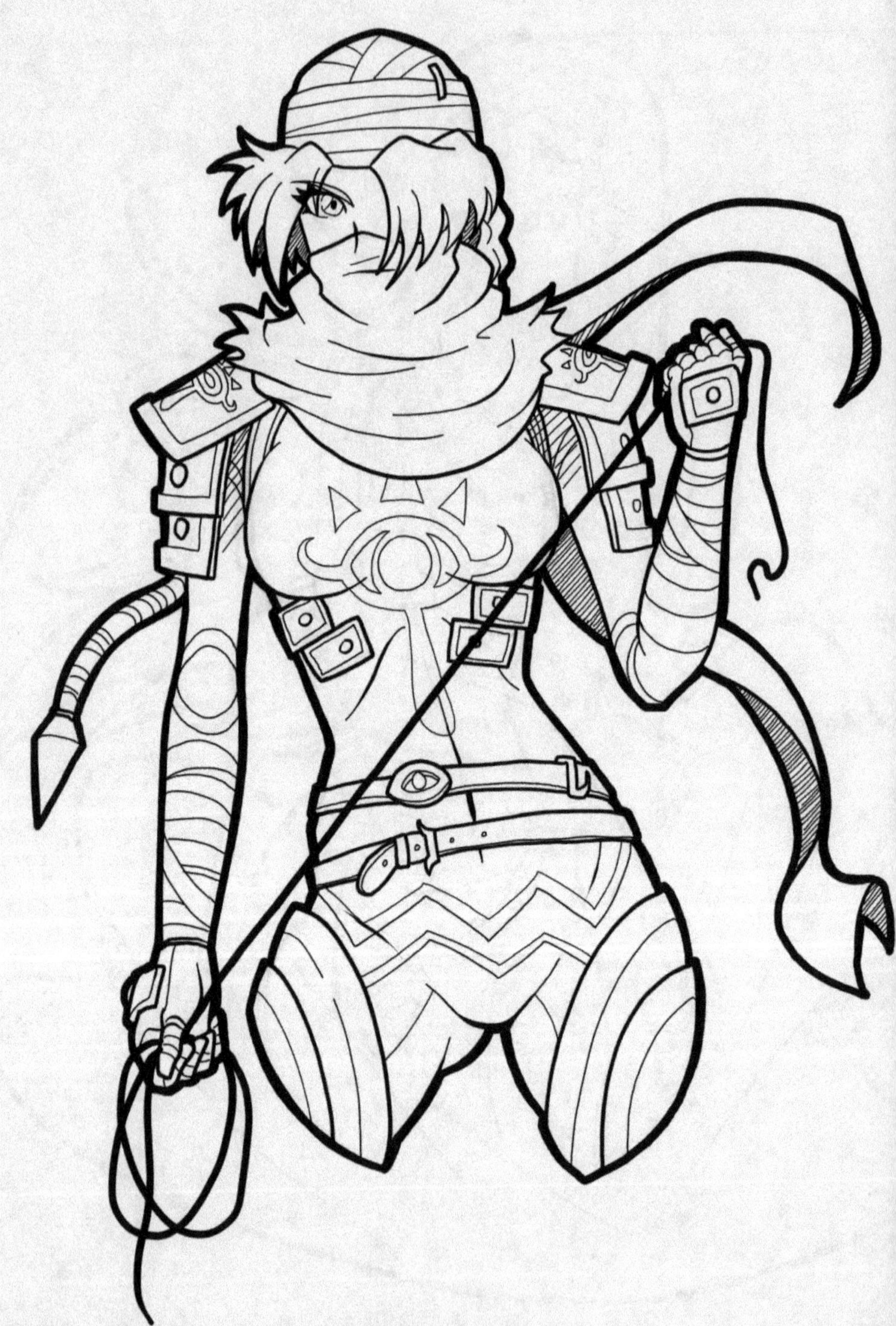

Sheik as depicted in *Super Smash Bros. Ultimate*

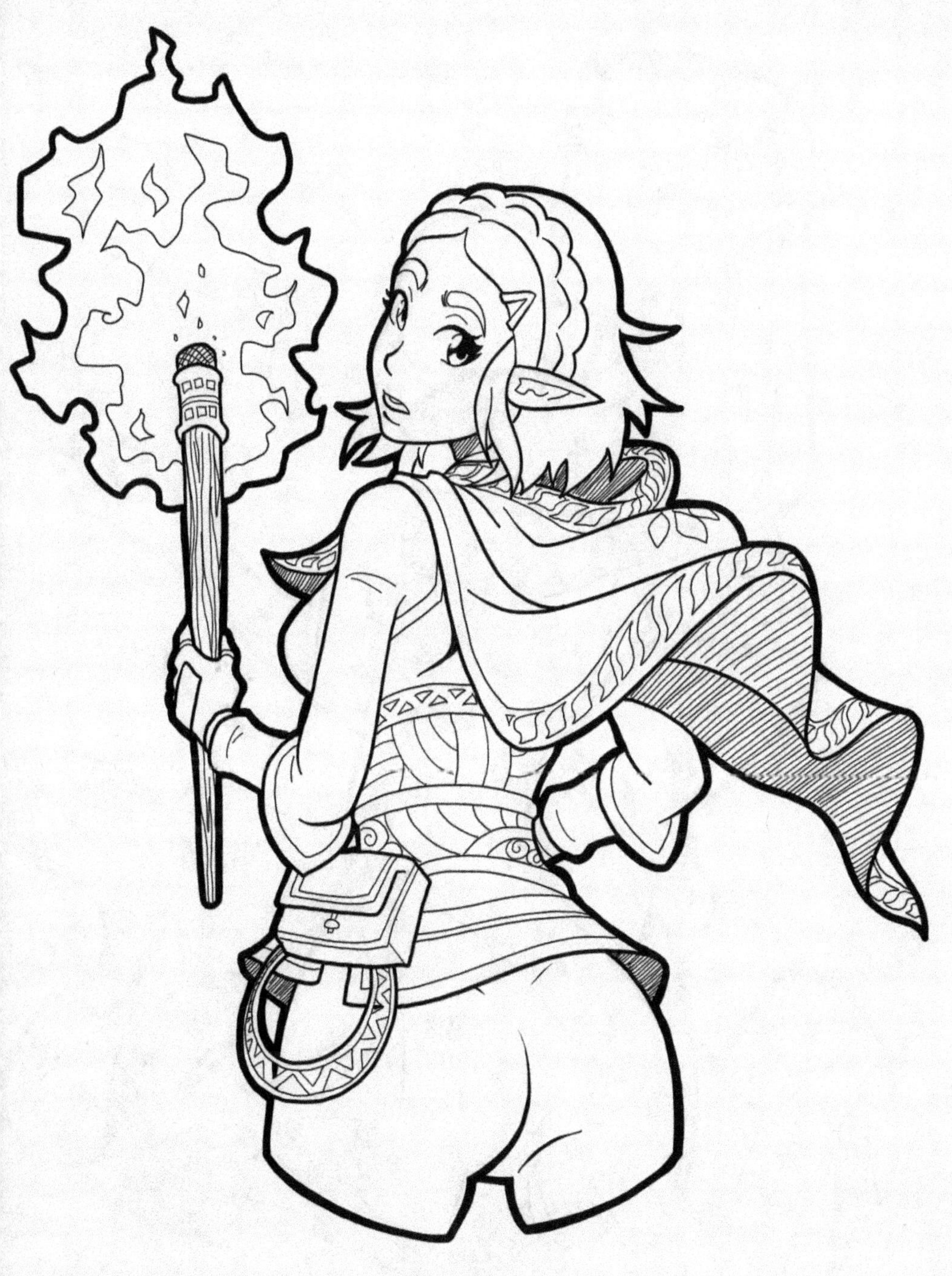

Princess Zelda as seen in *Tears of the Kingdom*

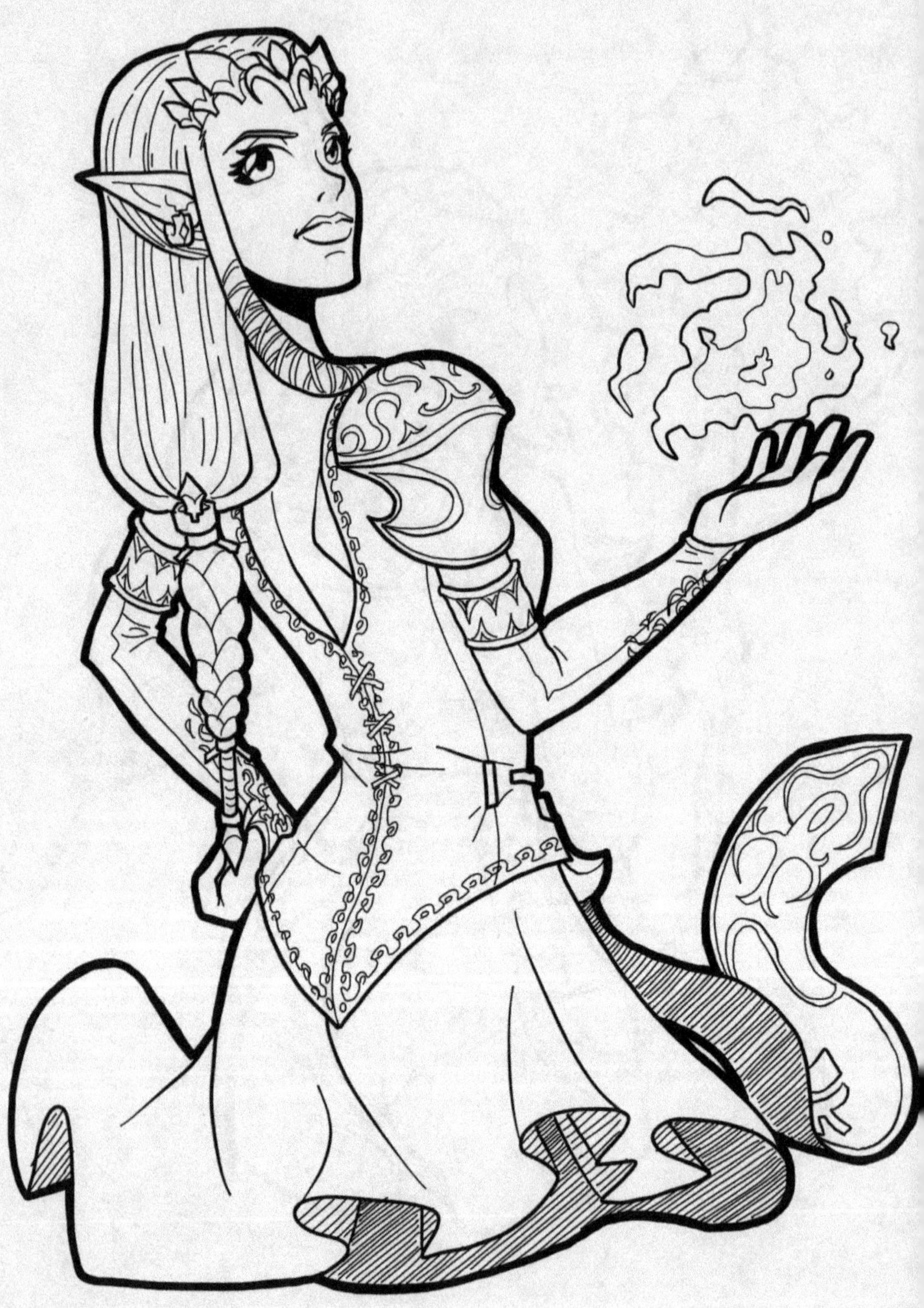

Princess Zelda from *Twilight Princess*

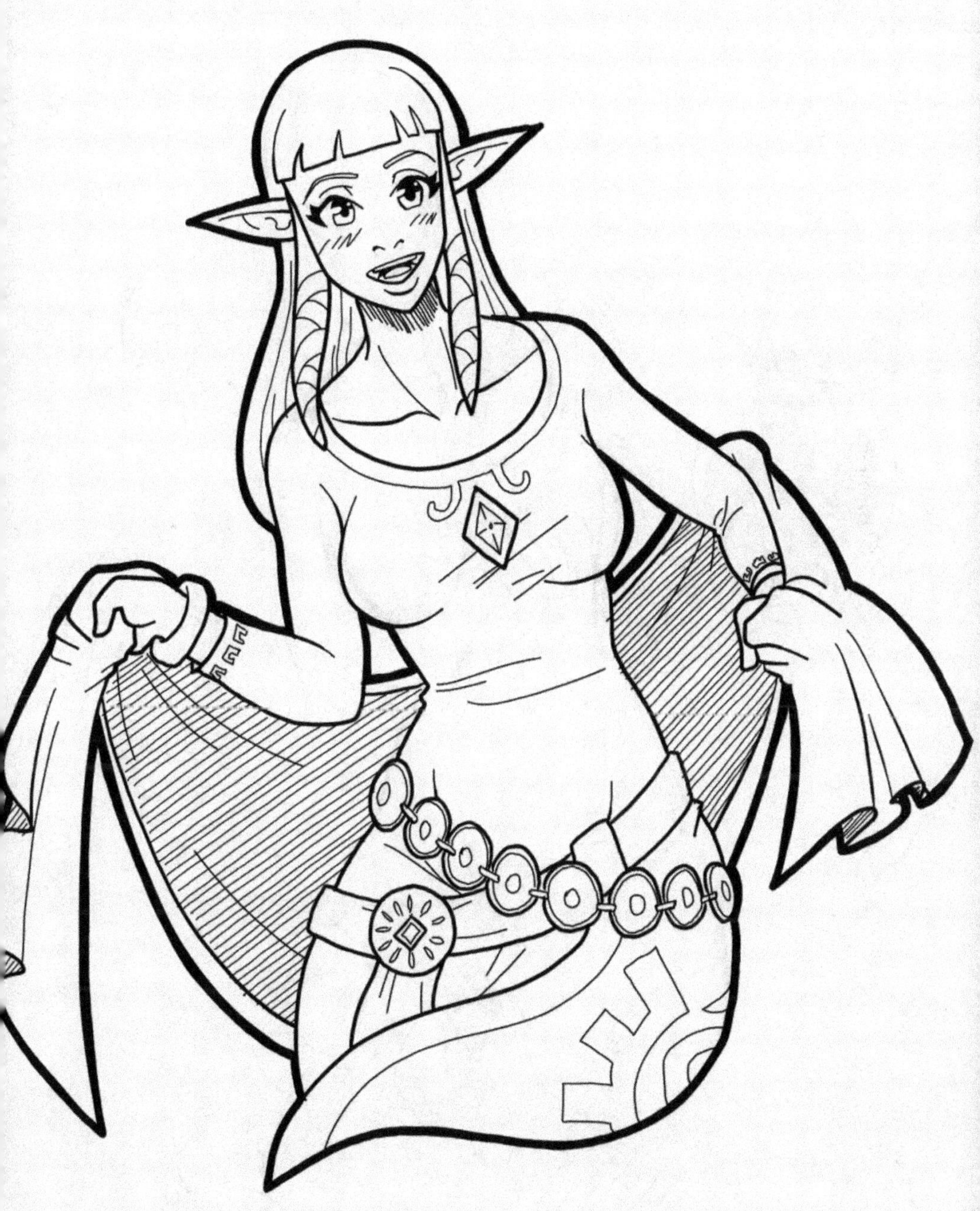

Zelda in her casual attire from *Skyward Sword*

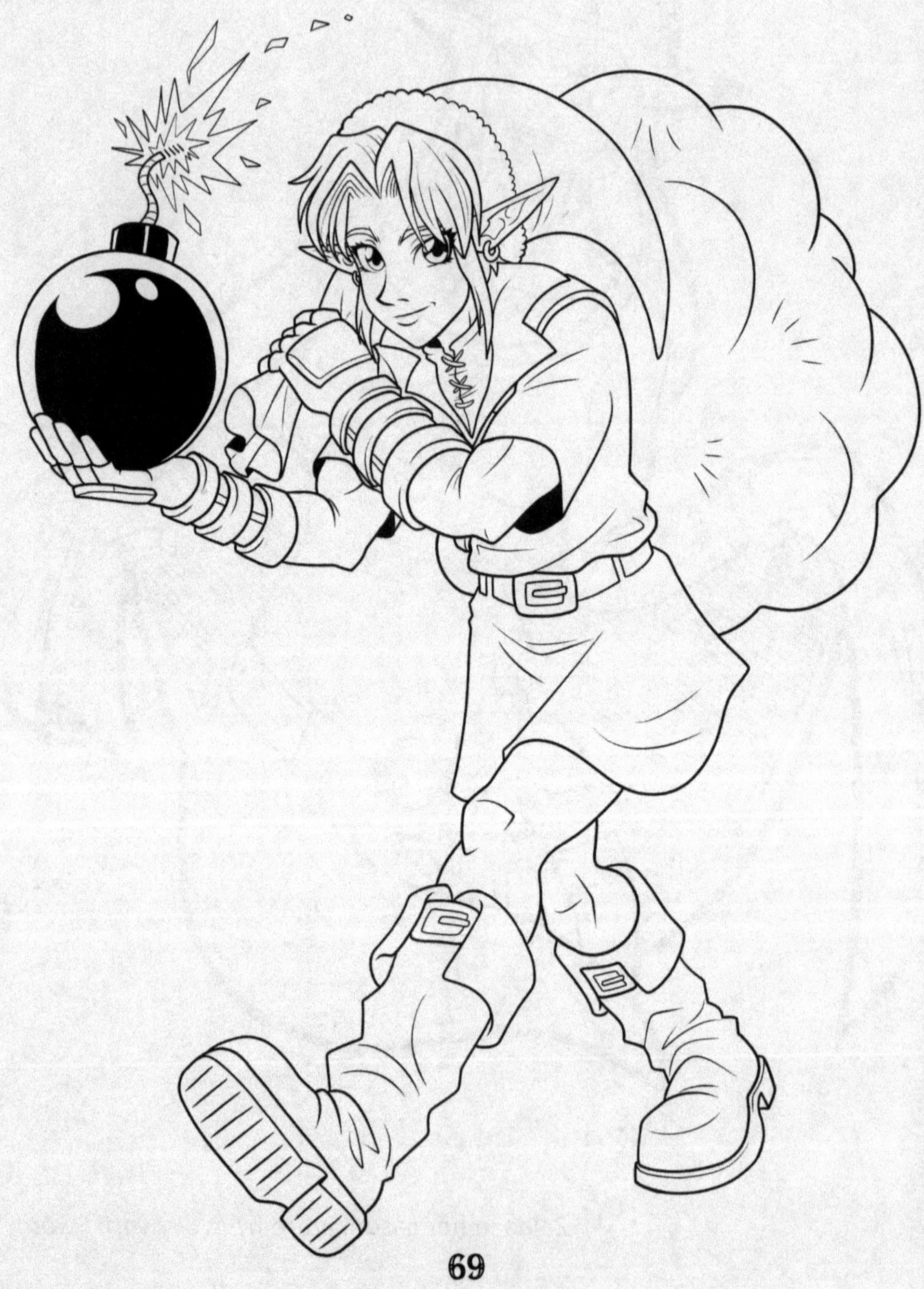

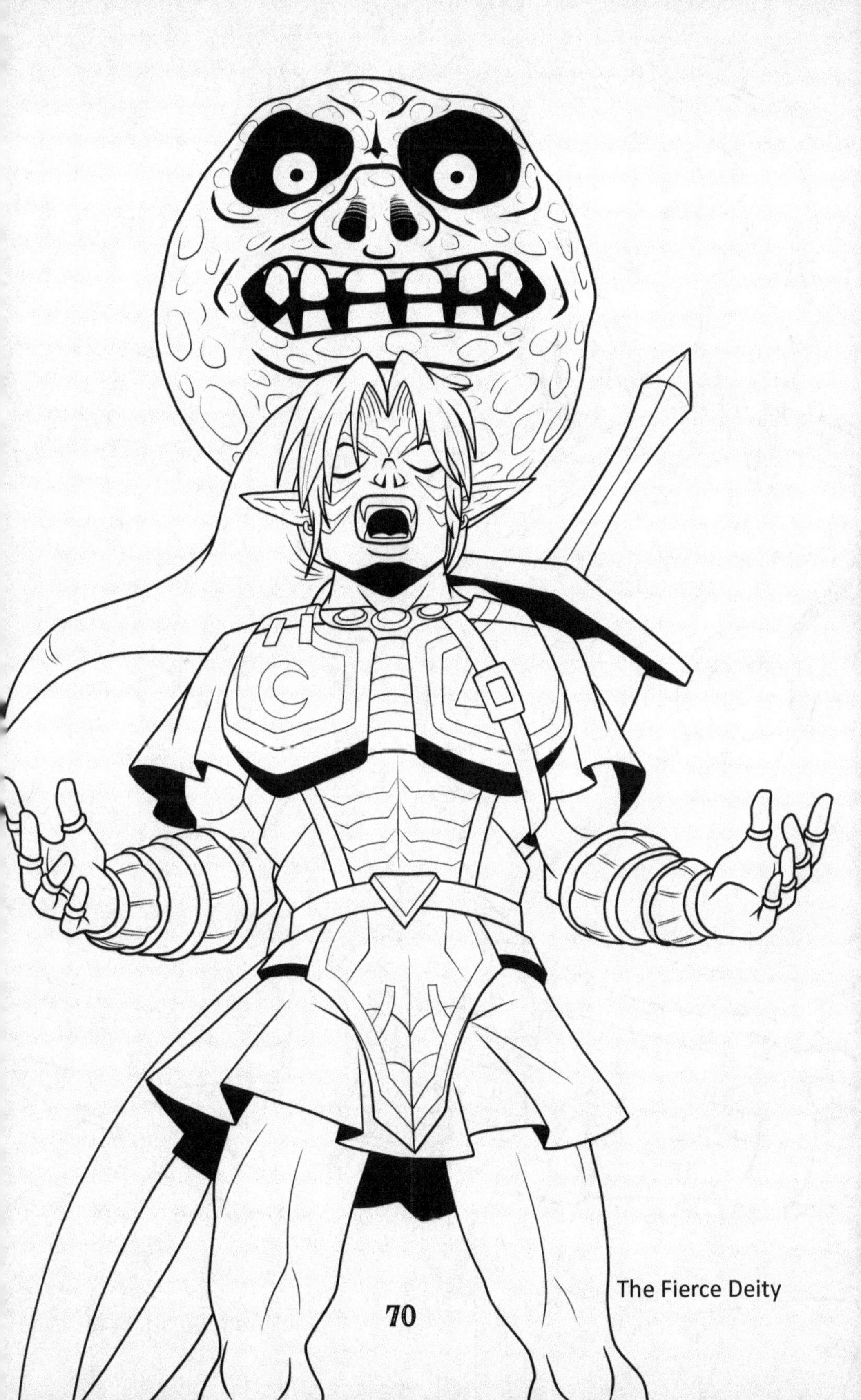

The Fierce Deity

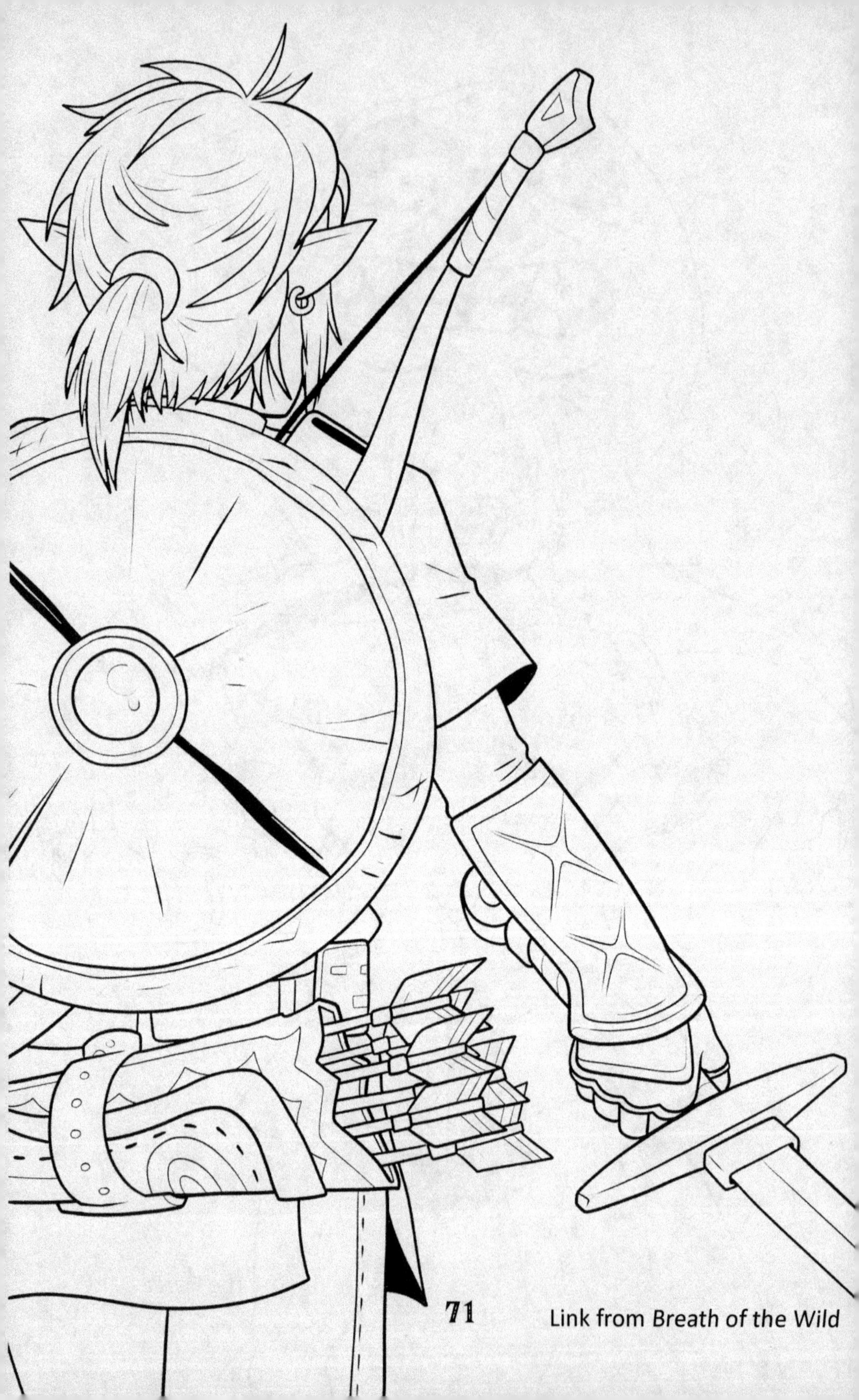

71

Link from *Breath of the Wild*

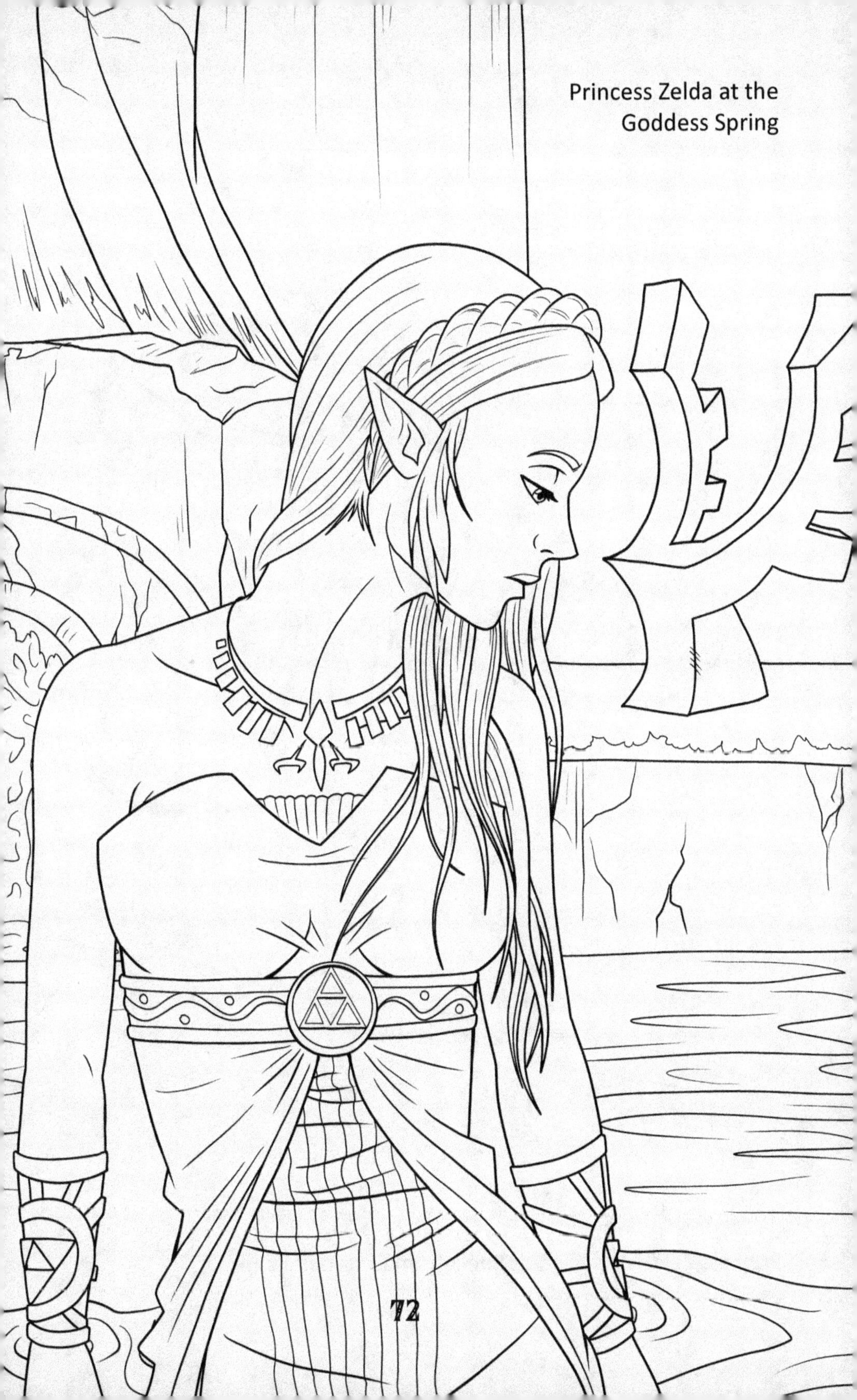

Princess Zelda at the
Goddess Spring

72

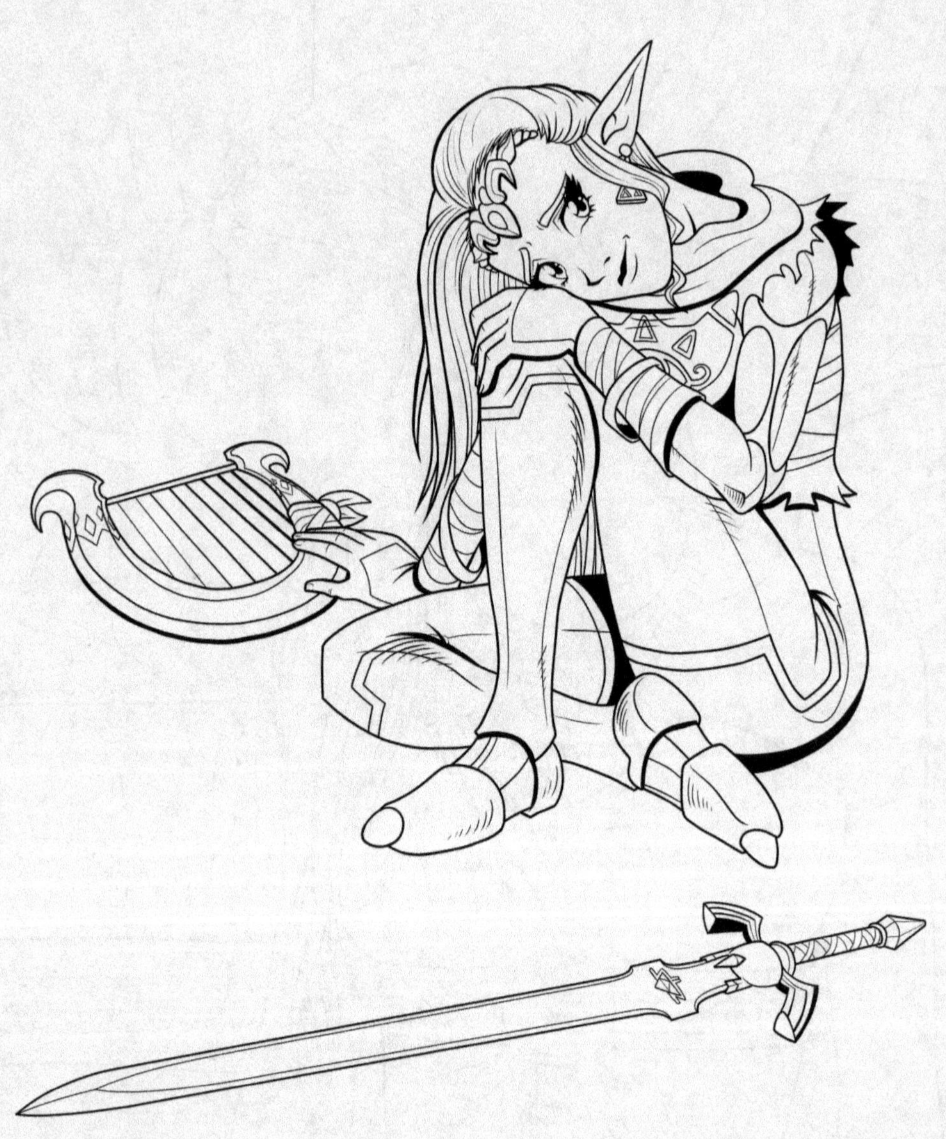

Princess Zelda disguised as Sheik from *Ocarina of Time*

Princess Zelda from *Breath of the Wild* taking a Sheikah Slate selfie

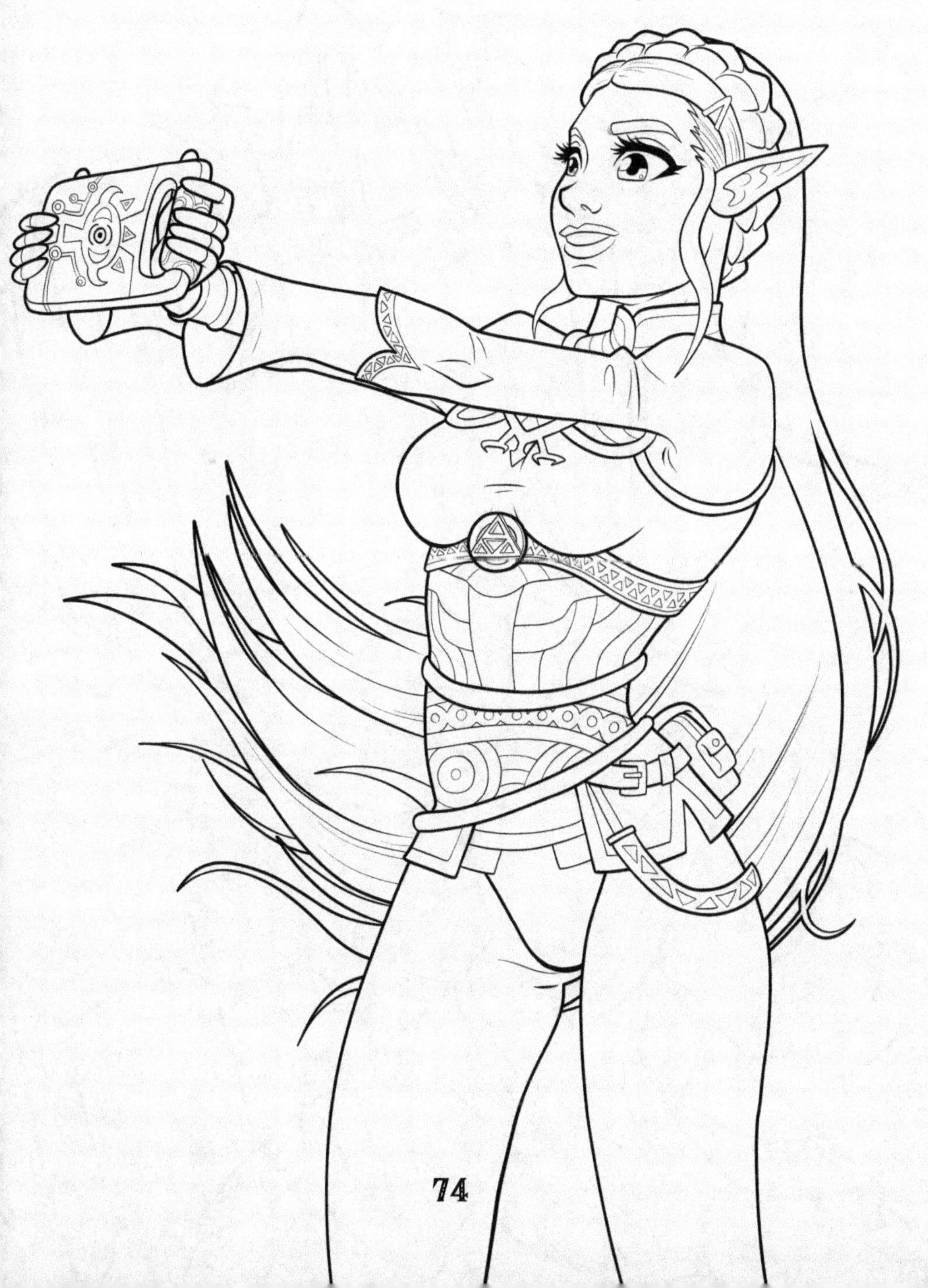

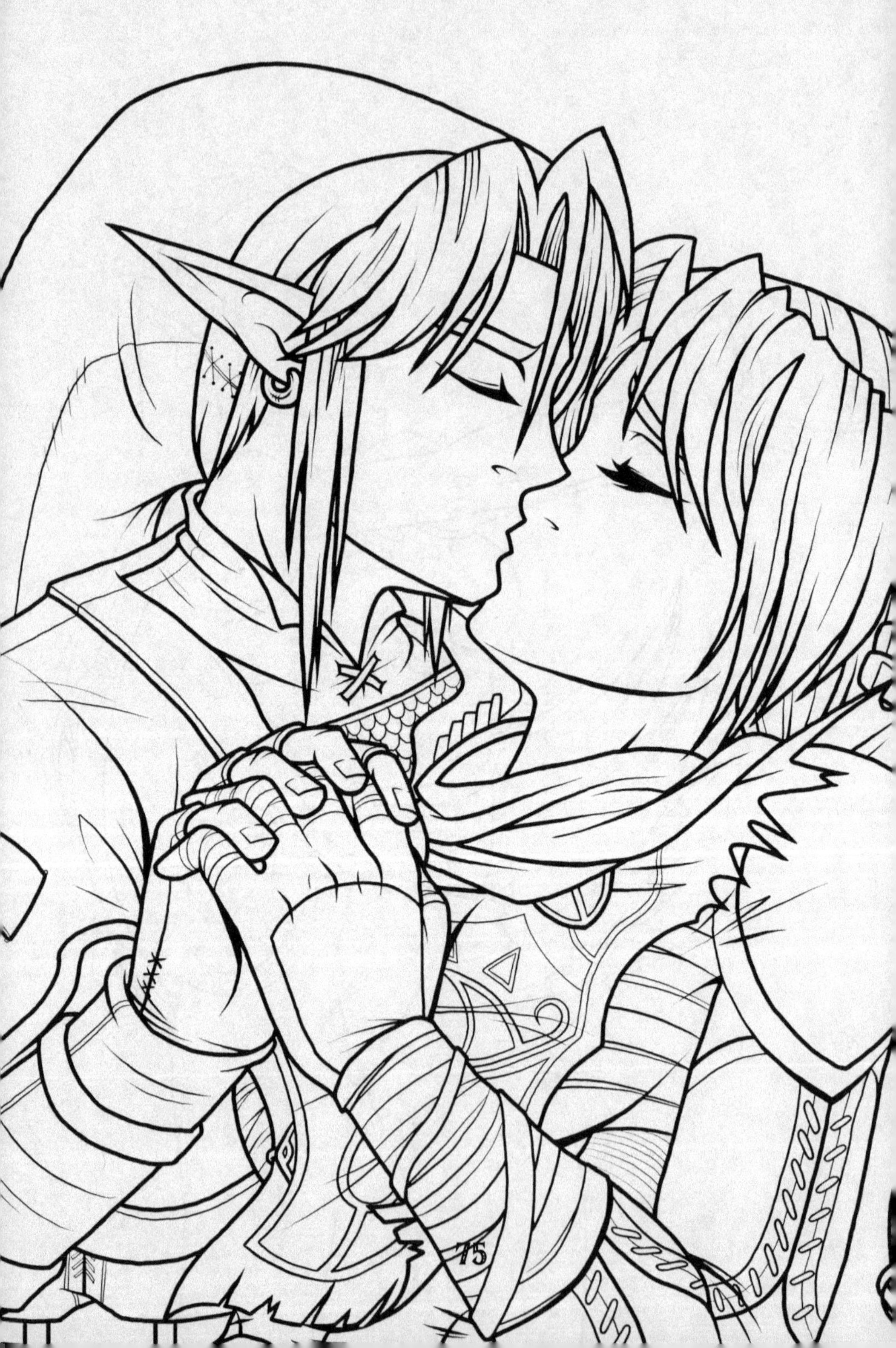

Link and Sheik/Zelda sharing a romantic kiss

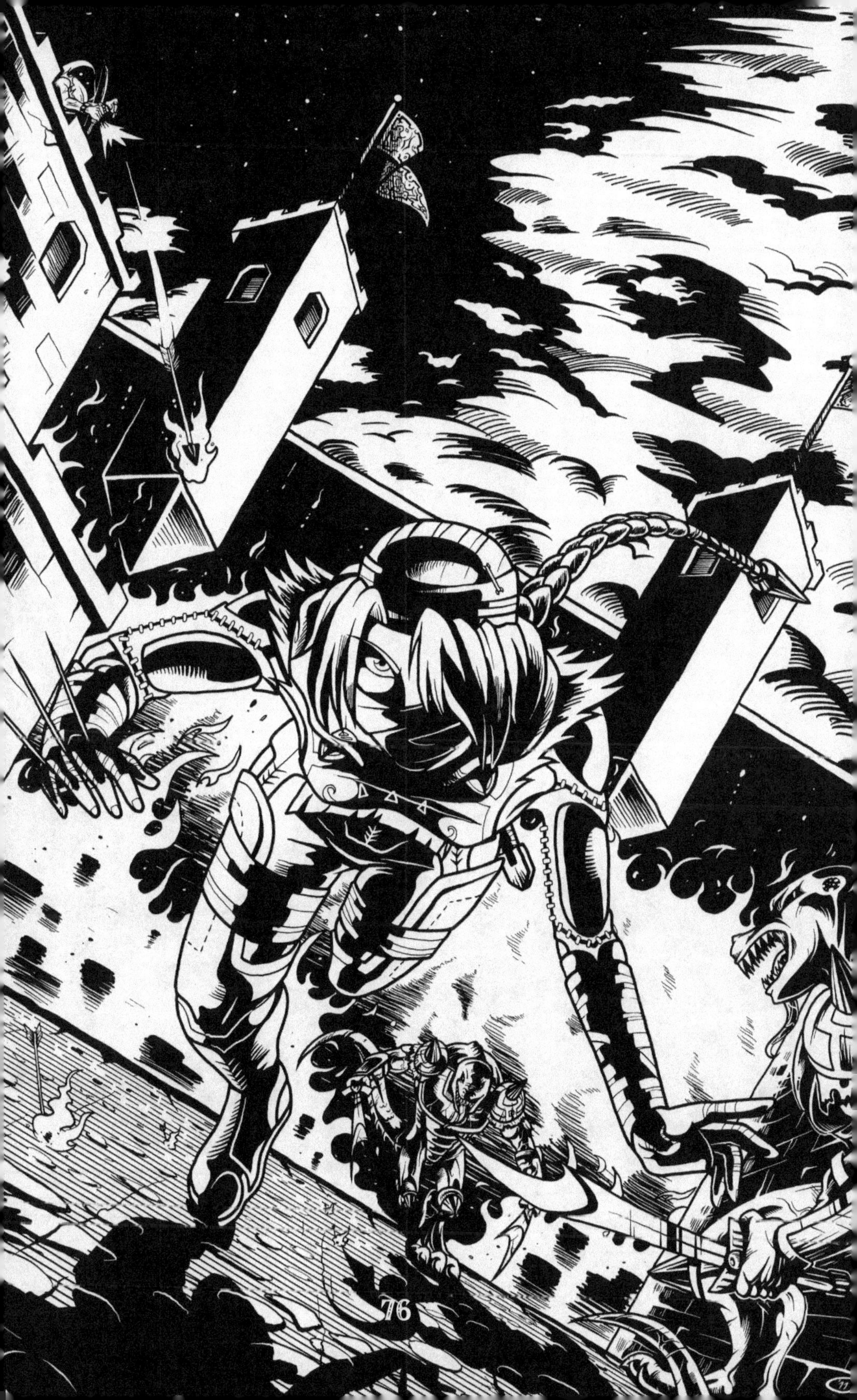

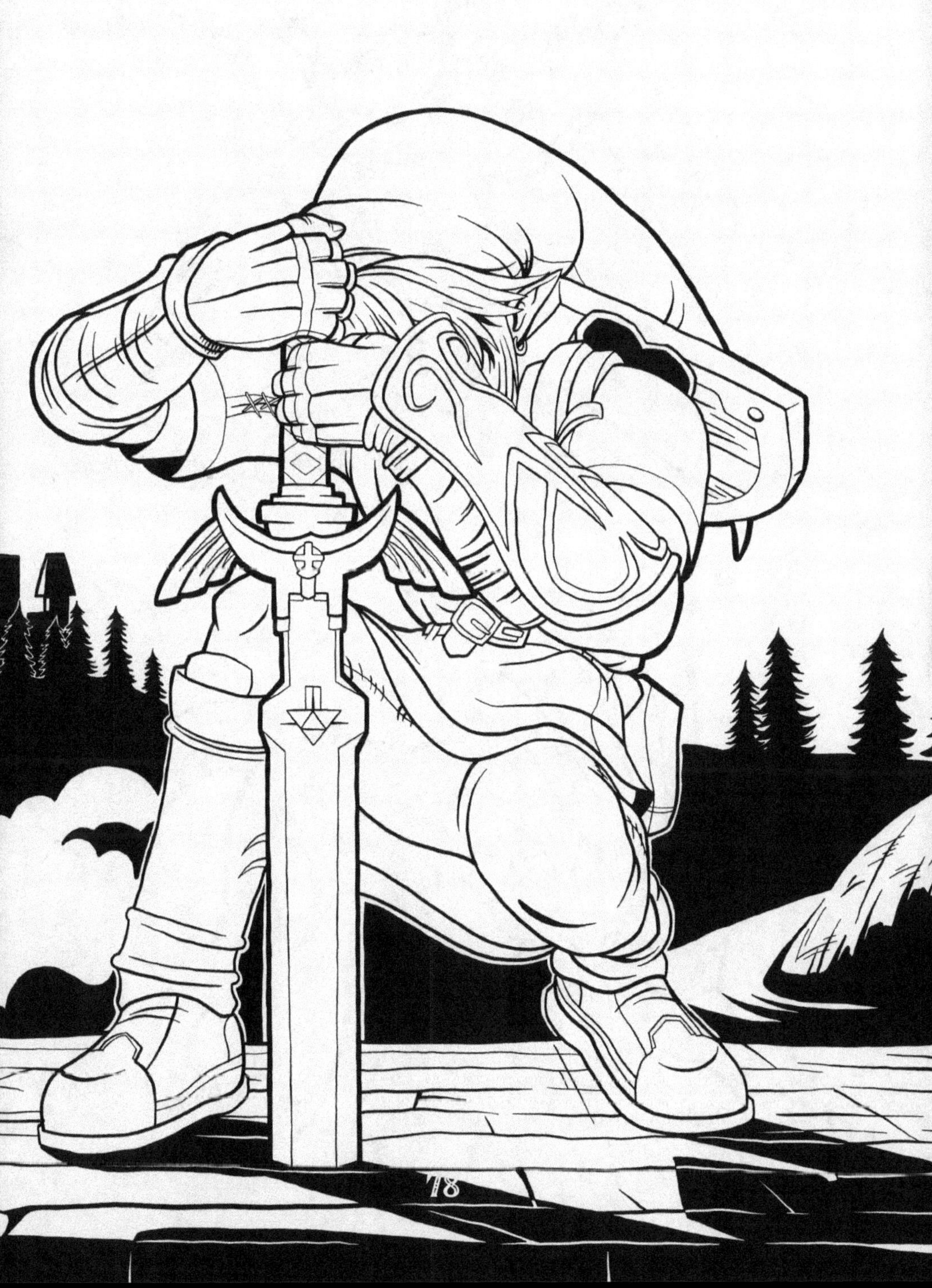

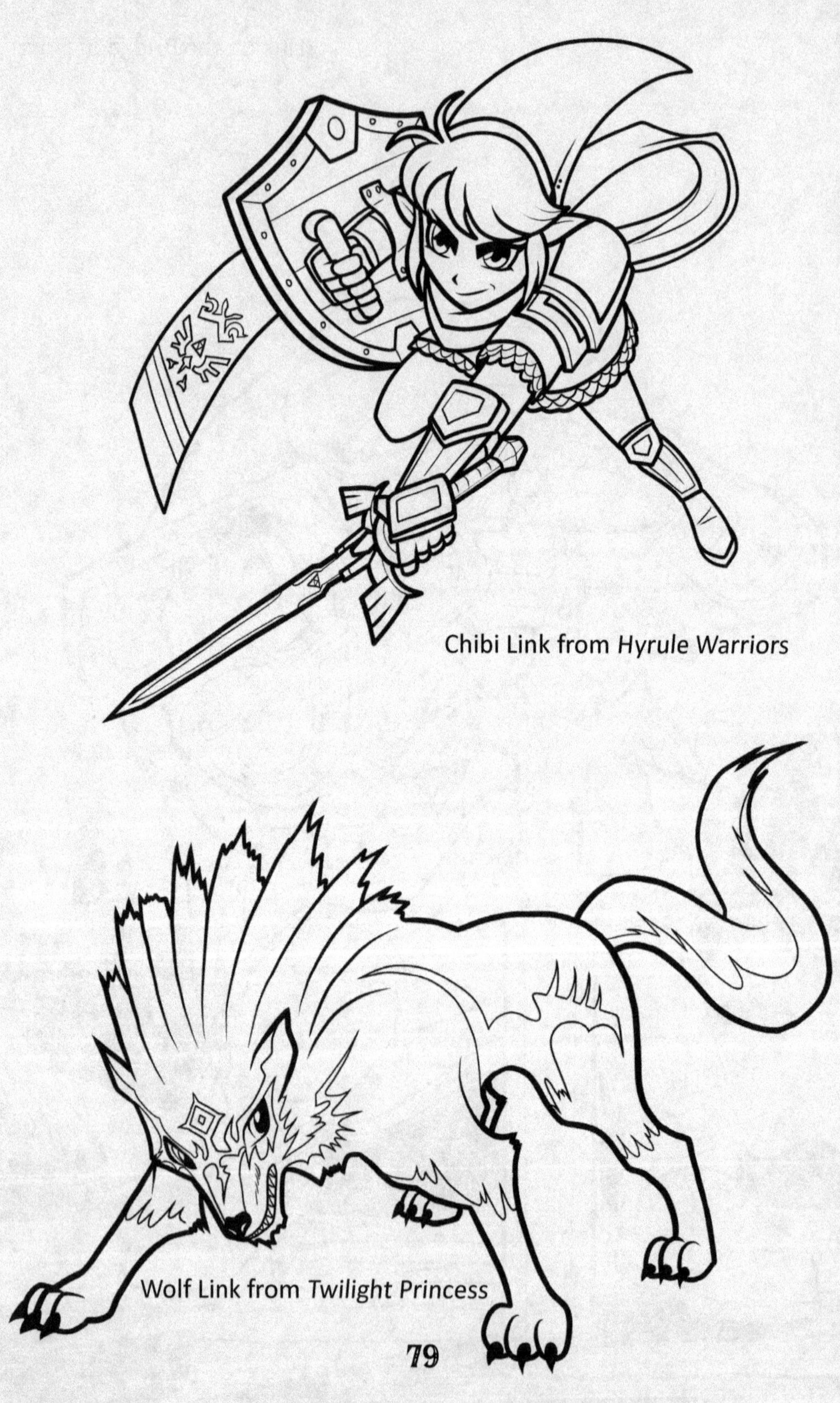

Chibi Link from *Hyrule Warriors*

Wolf Link from *Twilight Princess*

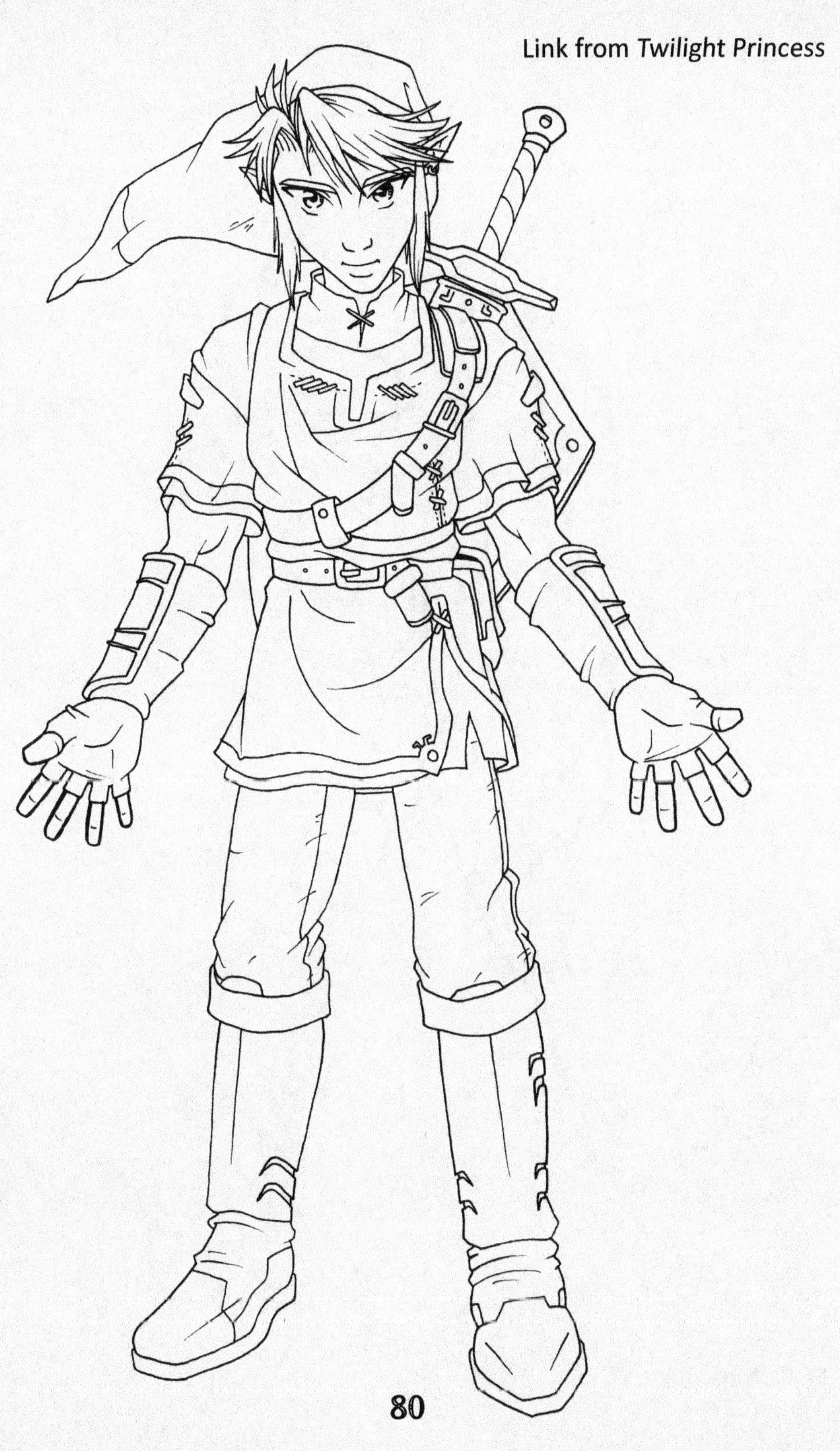

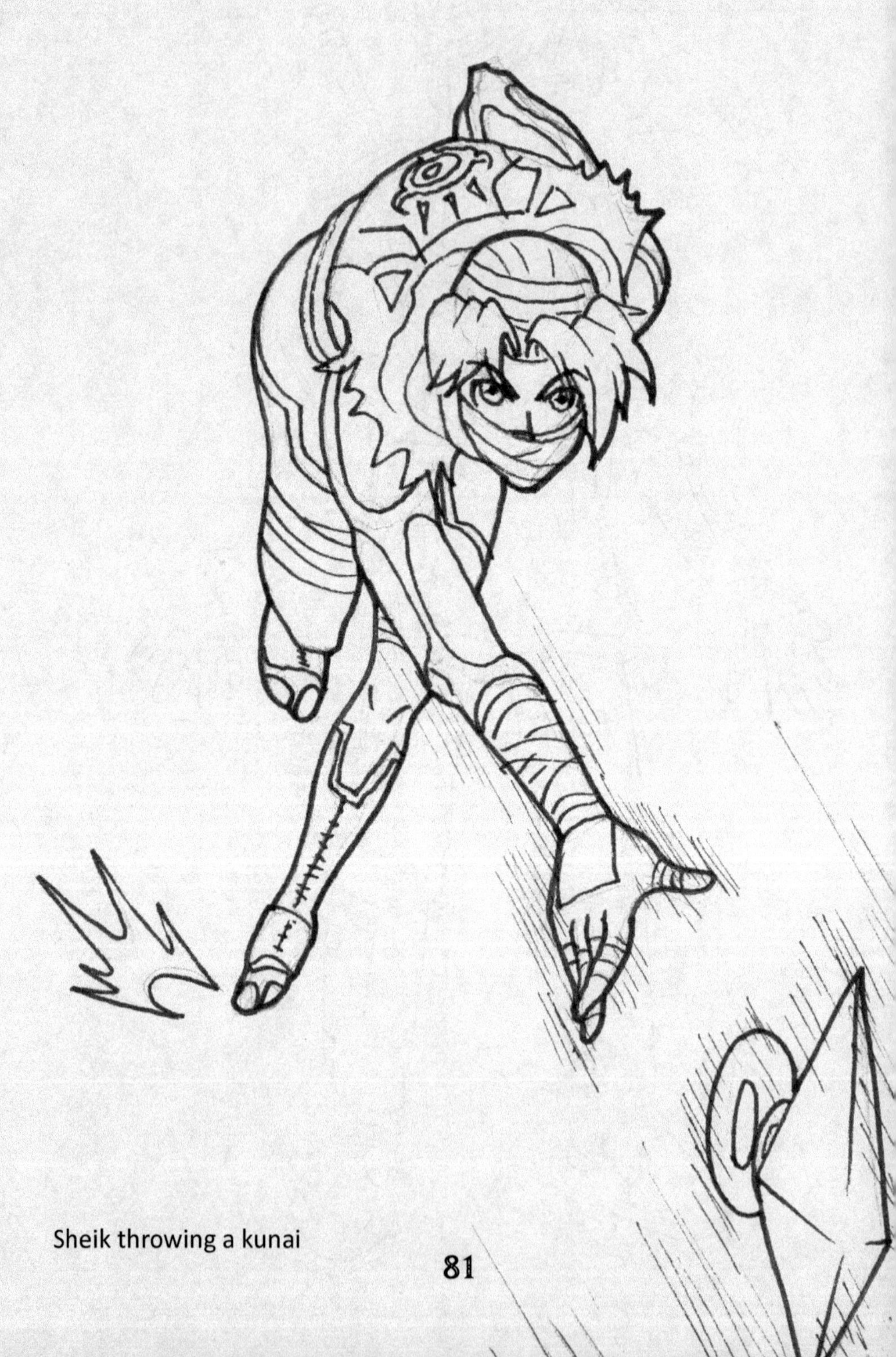

Sheik throwing a kunai

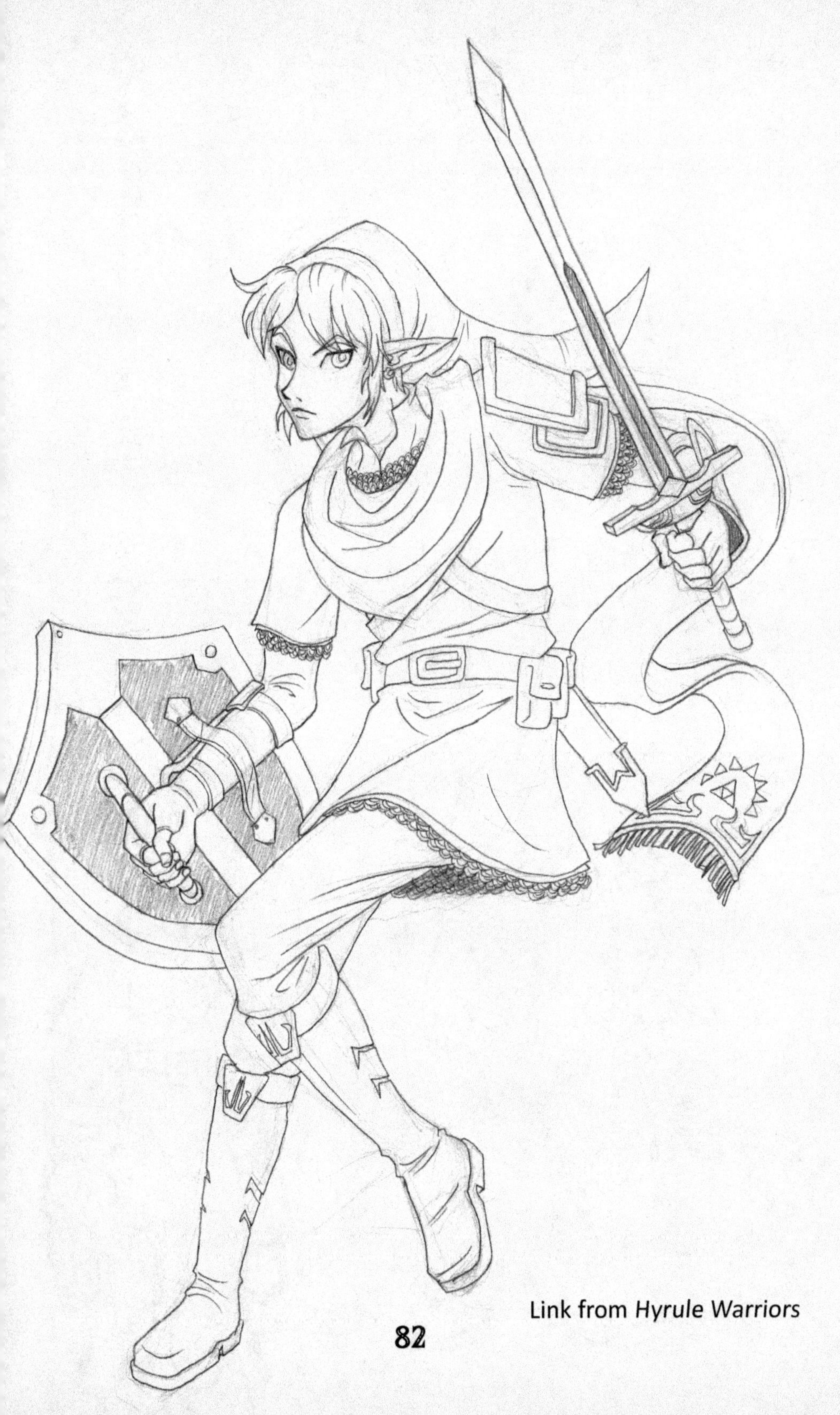

Link from Hyrule Warriors

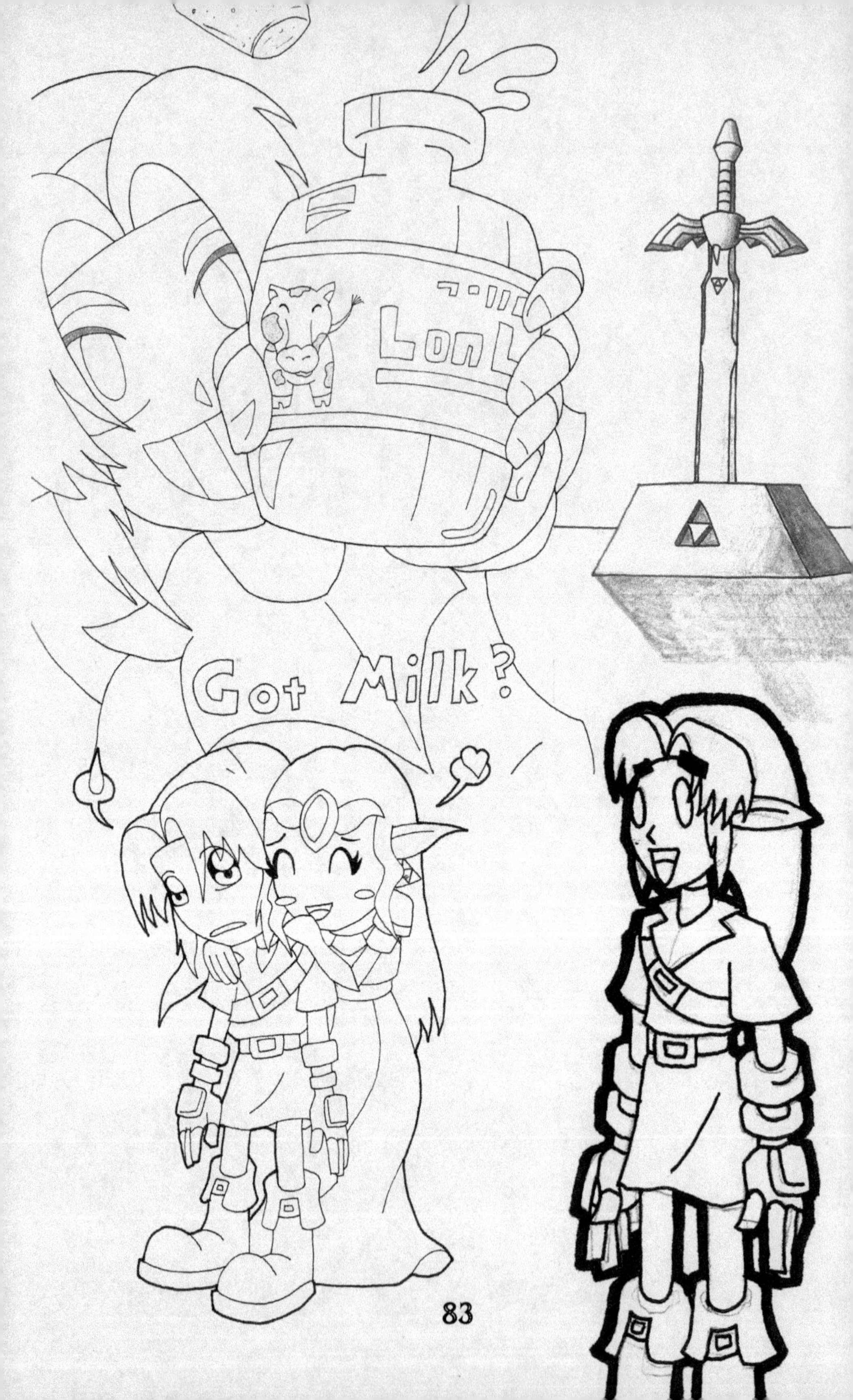
LonL
Got Milk?
83

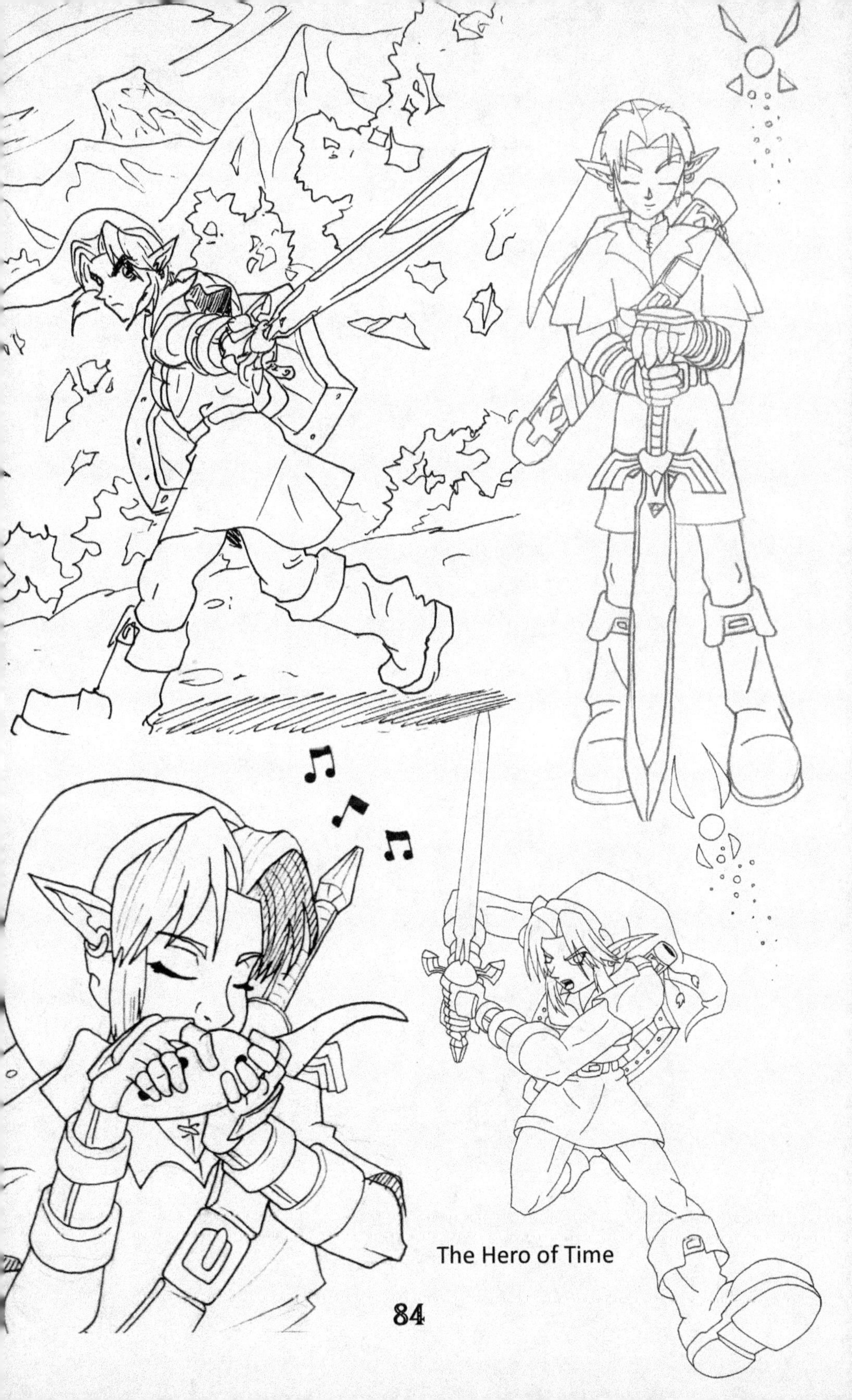

The Hero of Time

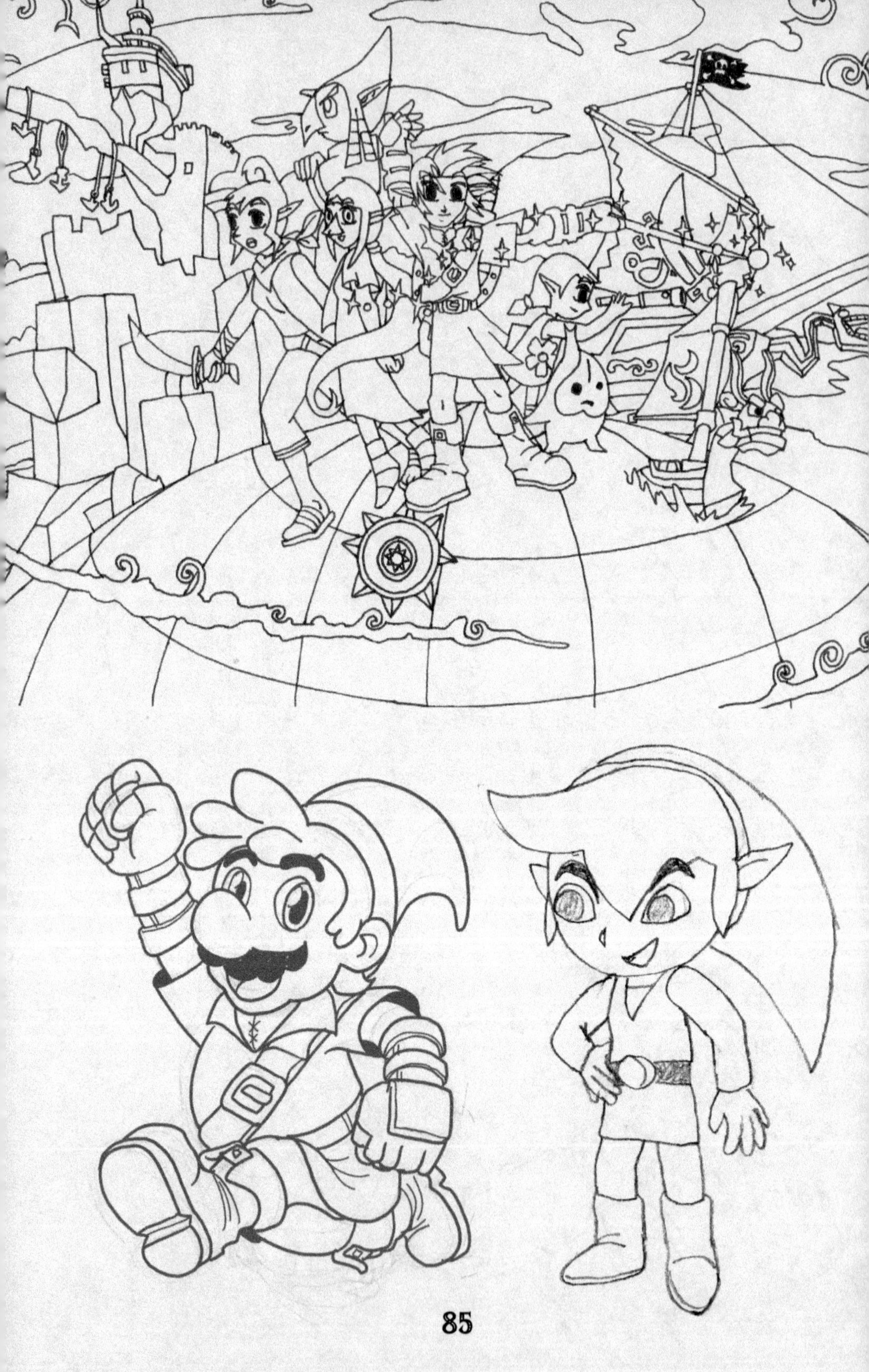

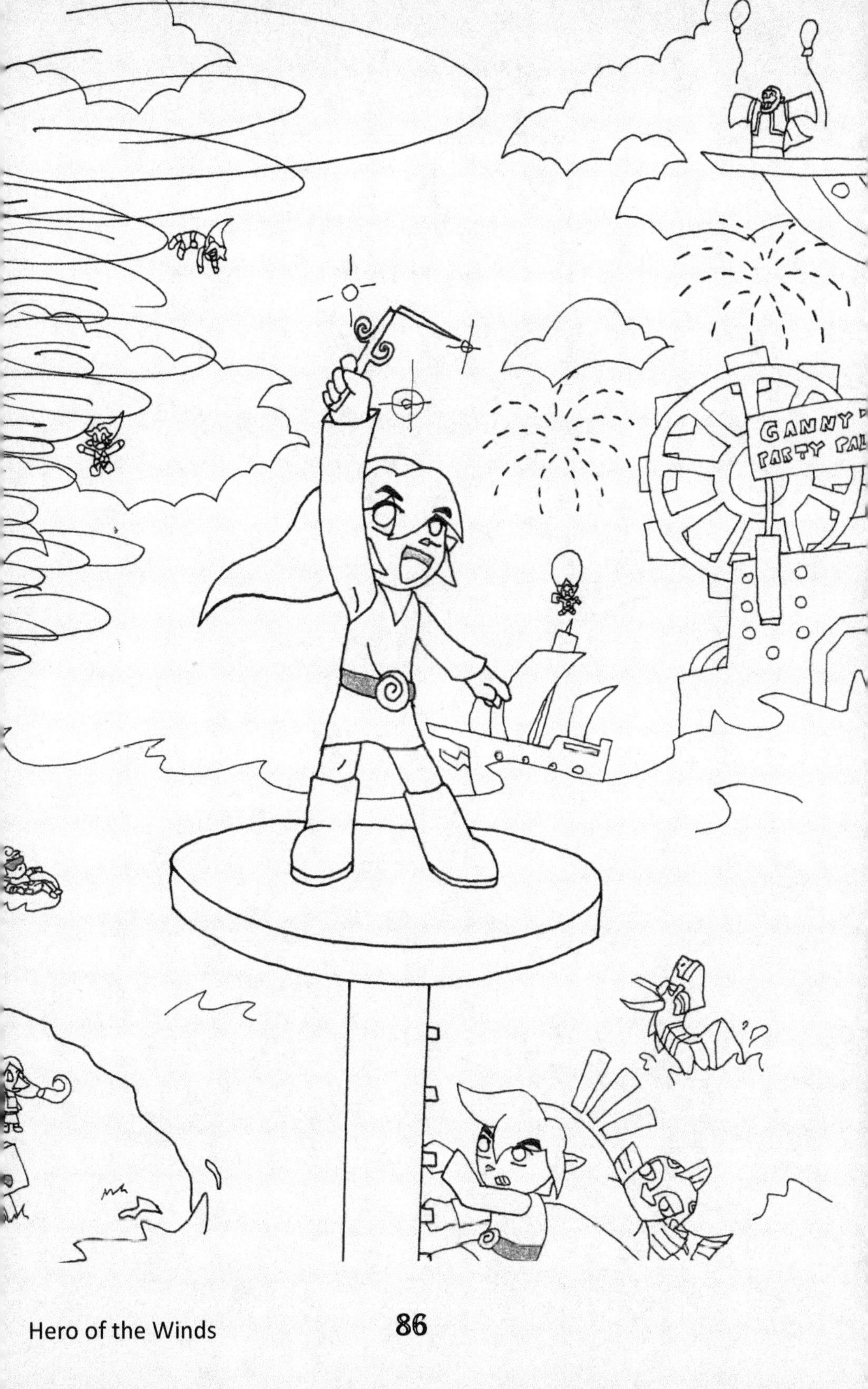

GANNY'
PARTY PAL

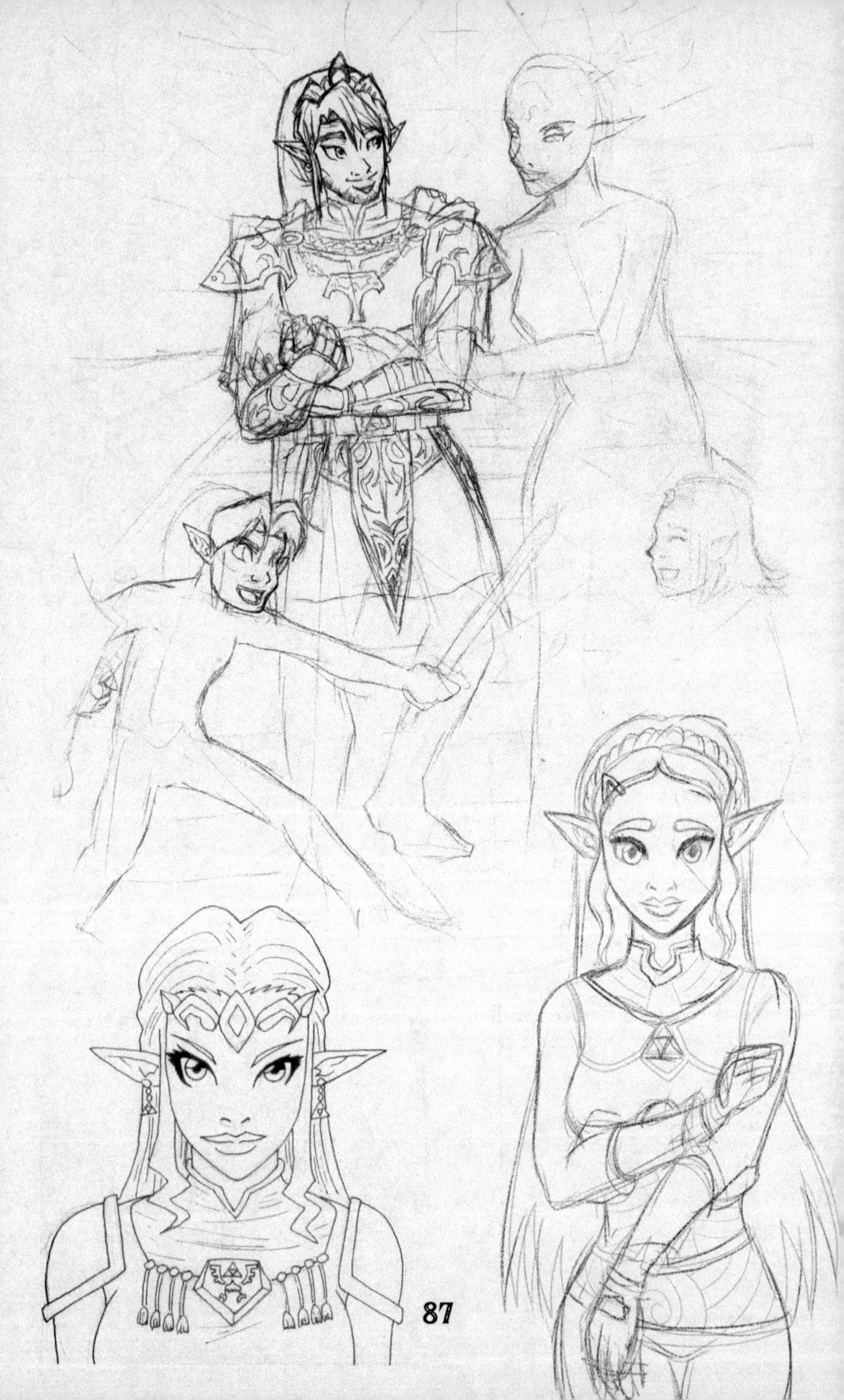

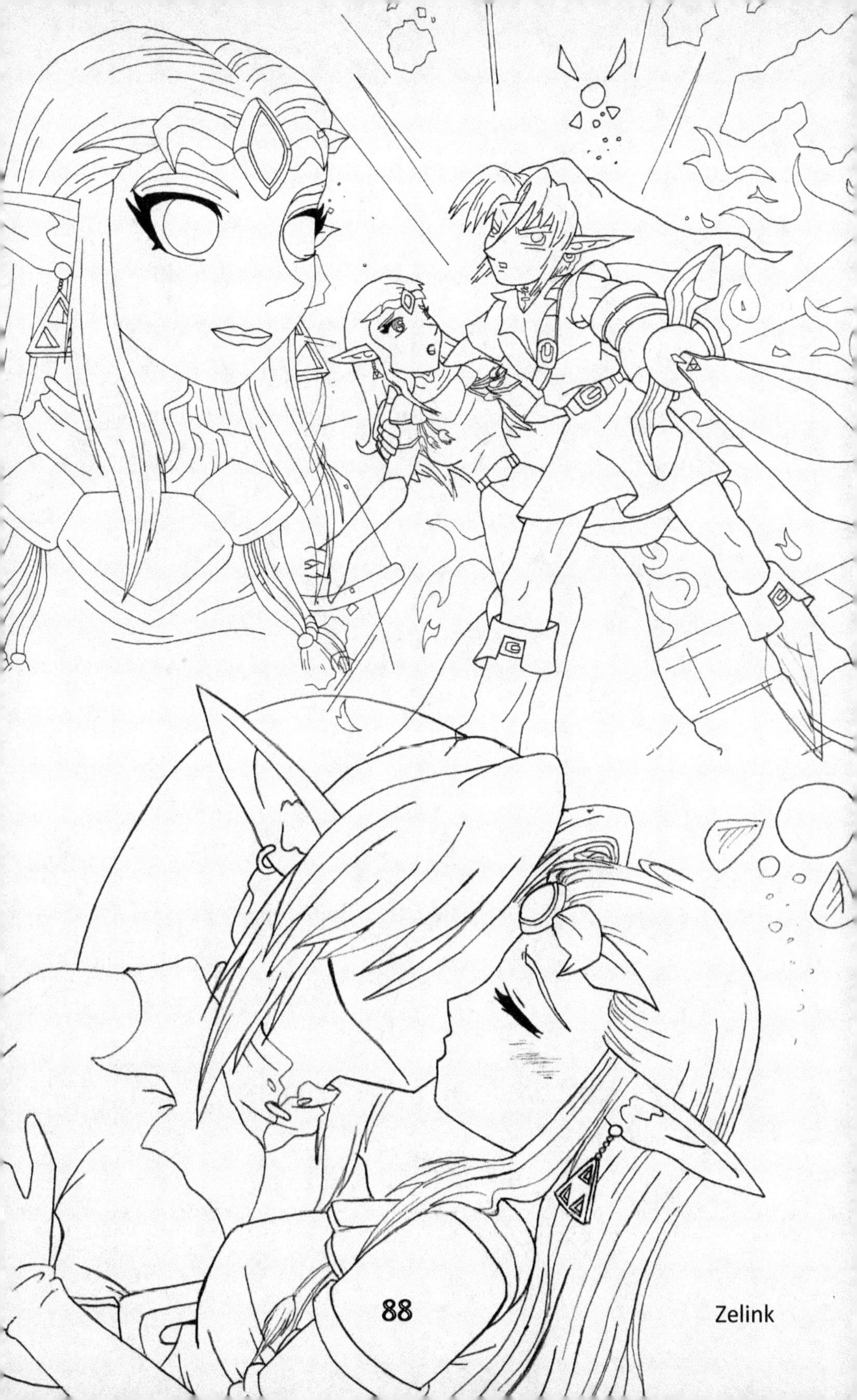

Zelink

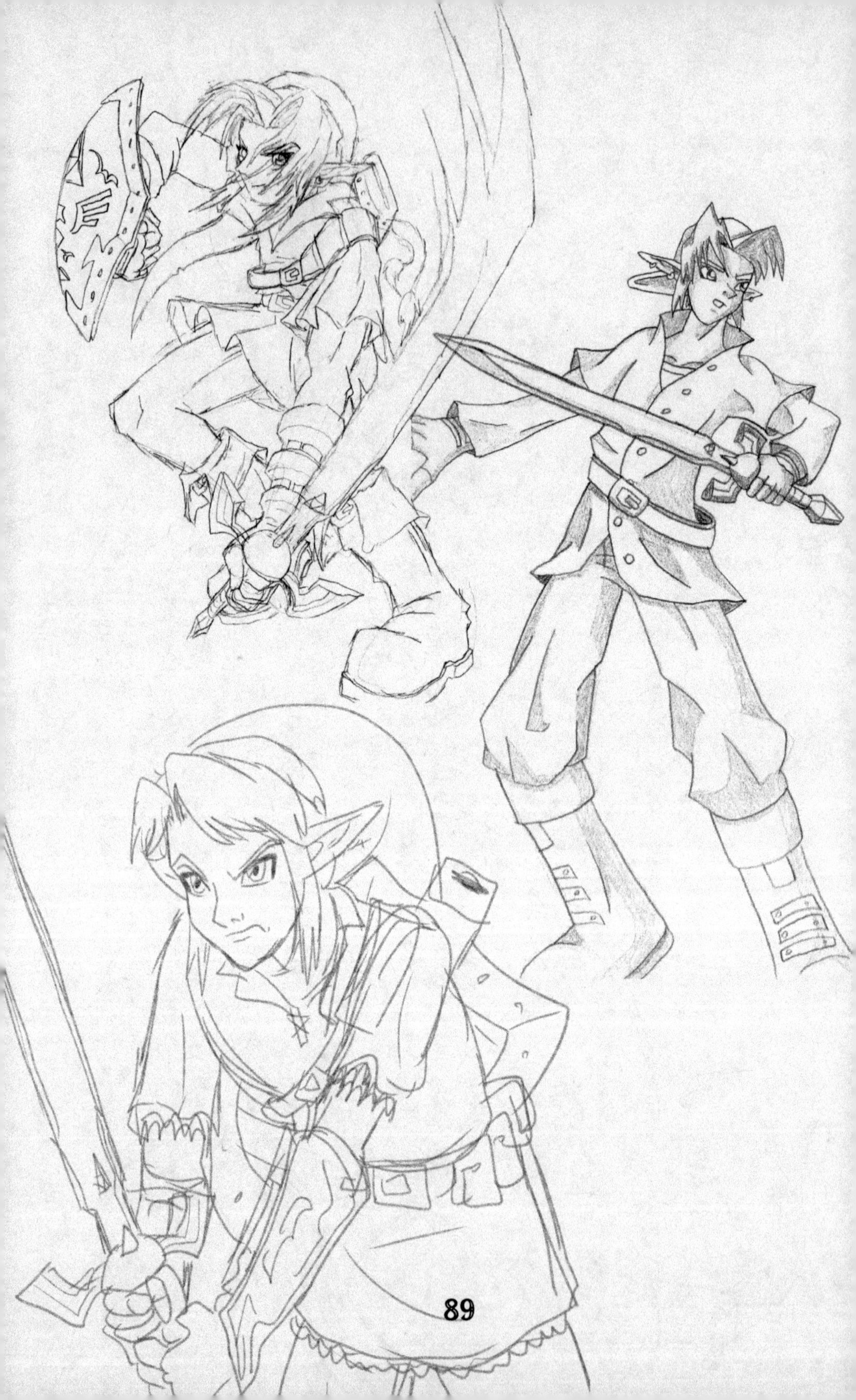

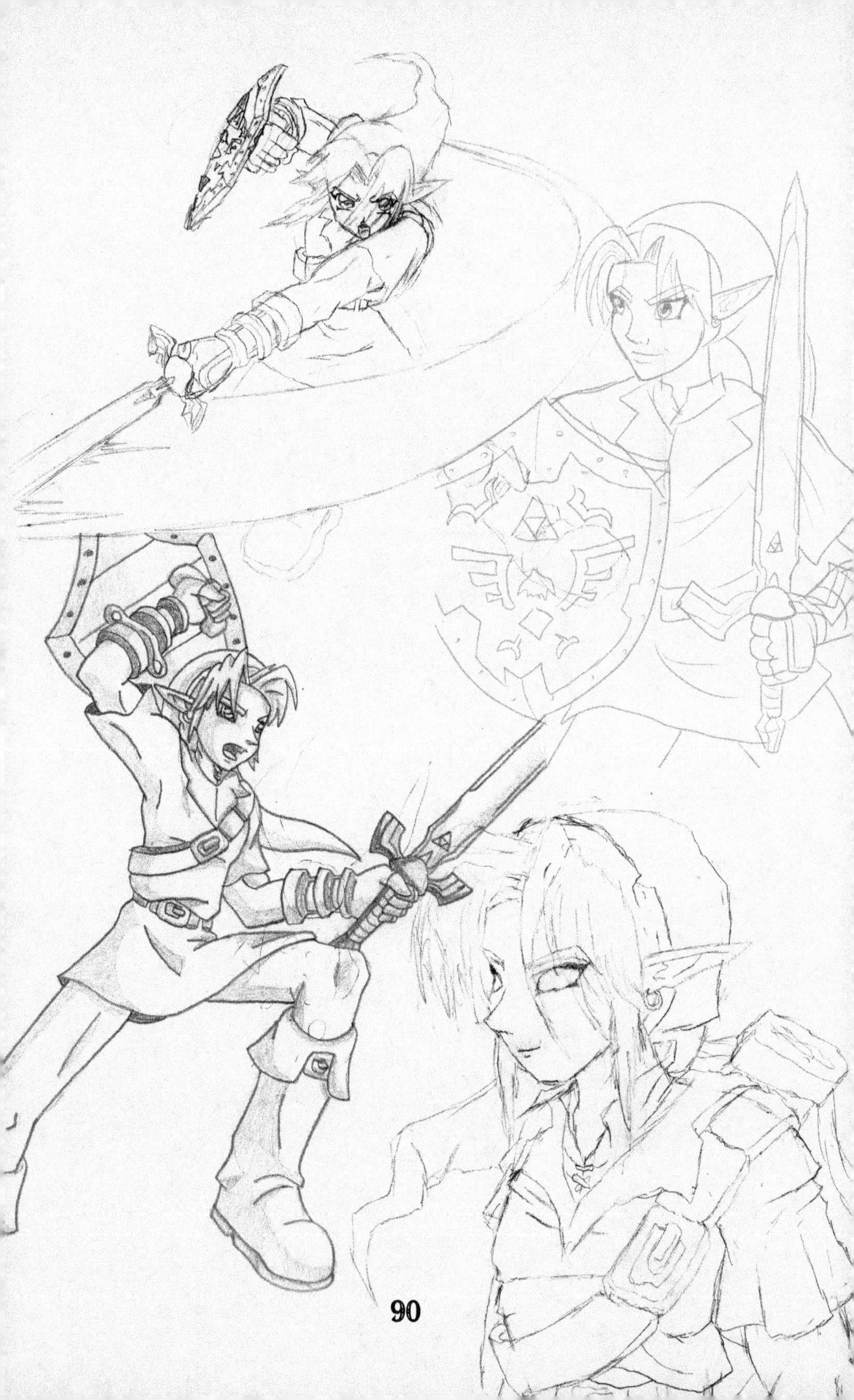

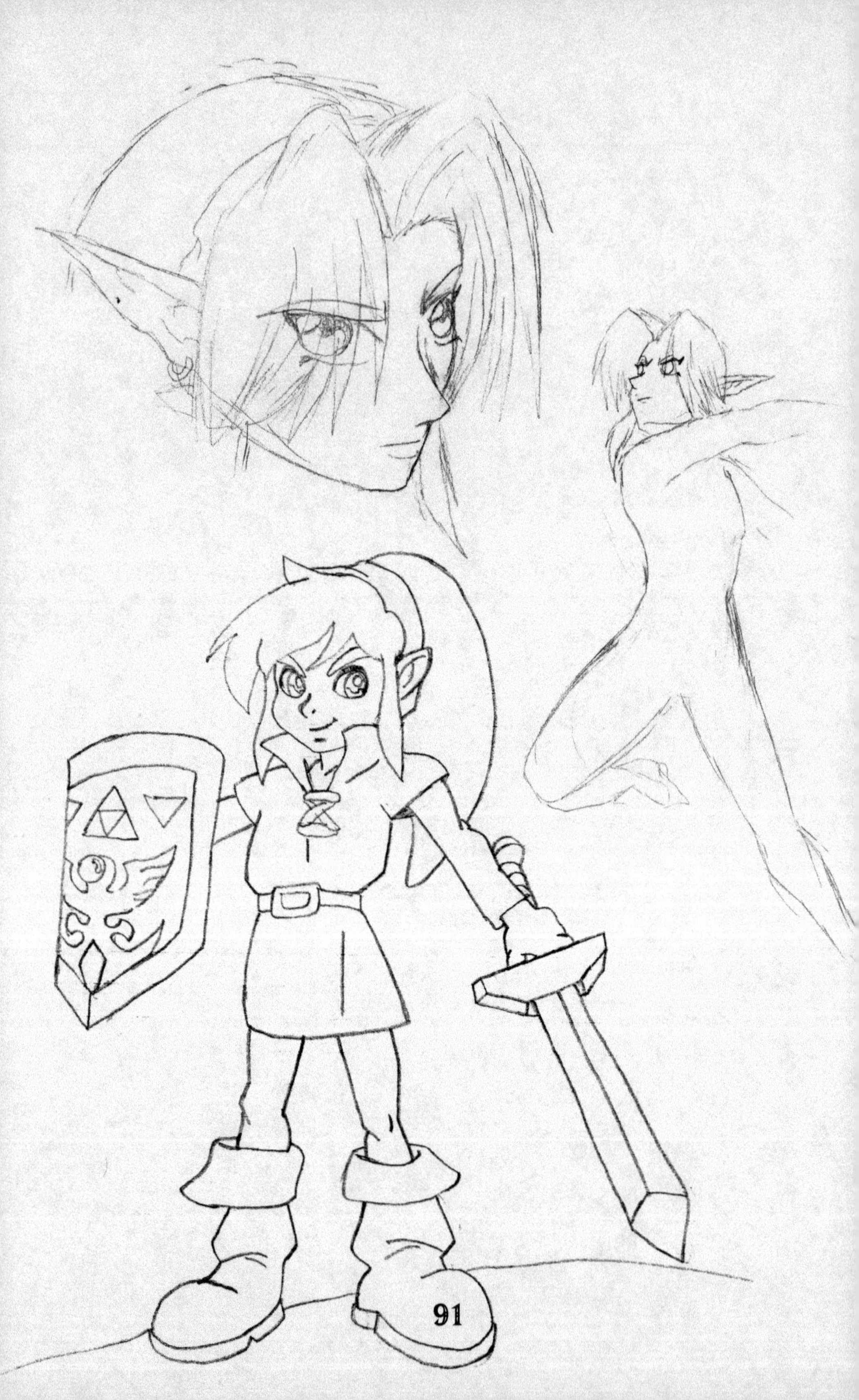

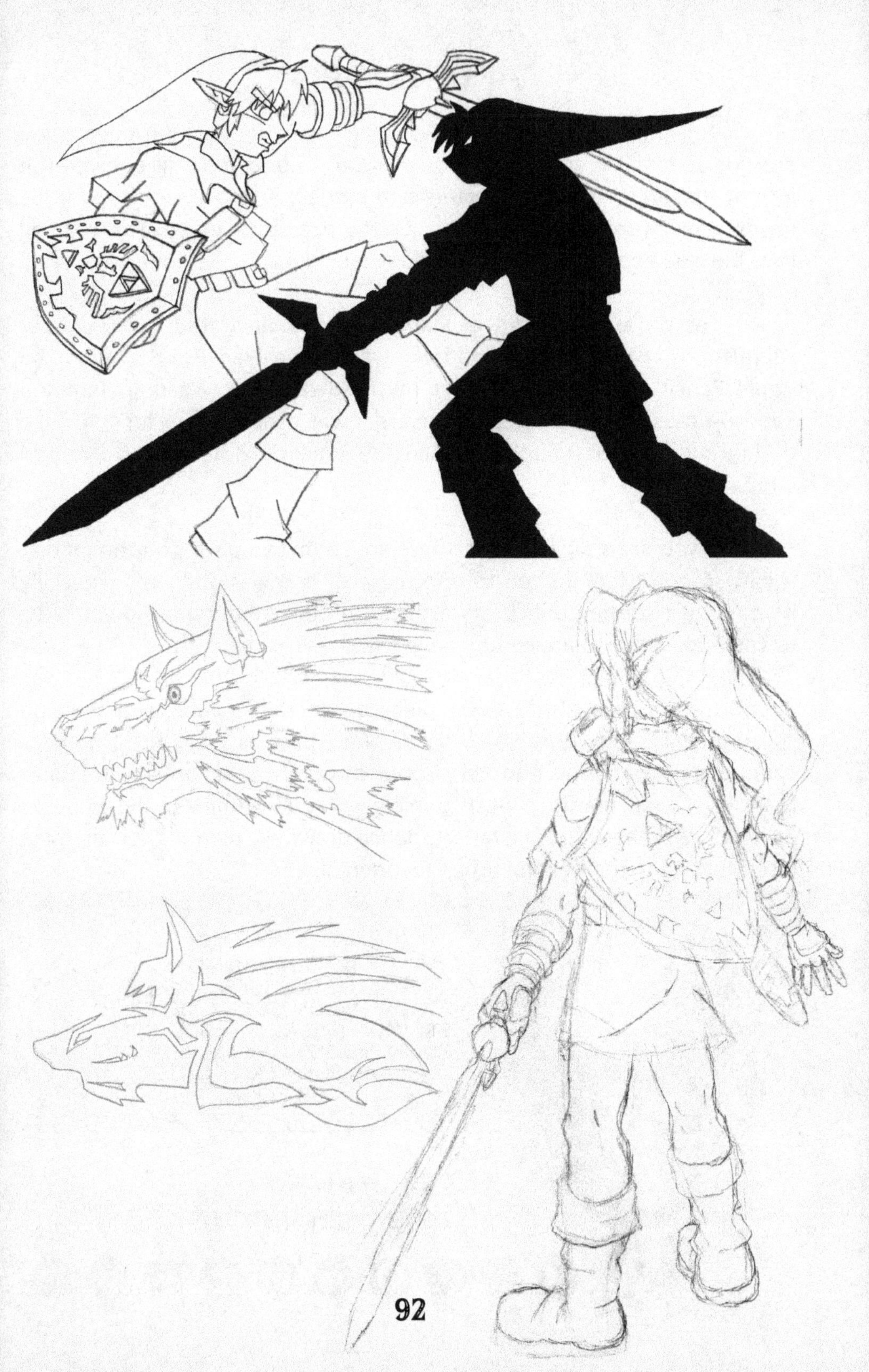

AFTERWORD

This book was made by a Zelda fan for Zelda fans! But even if you are not as familiar with the series as I am, I hope you still enjoyed the lore of these fantastical characters and stories. At the very least, I hope my drawings were enough to warrant a thumbs up! To every artist reading this, please keep drawing and consider taking part of Inktober this year!

For those interested in learning how I illustrated my Linktober submissions, I used a combination of an Apple iPad Pro 12" with the Apple Pencil (2nd Generation) as my hardware and Wacom's Bamboo Paper App as my drawing software. This was a new setup for me since during my previous Inktober I used the Wacom Mobilestudio Pro and Clip Studio Paint.

If you are a digital artist, there are so many options on the market today, so don't feel limited to one piece of hardware or app, especially if you're just starting out. Every artist's journey is different and you have to you find what you are comfortable with!

It is my hope that every piece of art that I publish or post on social media inspires others to create and share as well. The Linktober community is amazing and very supportive, as is the original Inktober team. We're all trying to push ourselves, try new things, and improve our craft, whether it be digital art, pencil drawings, painting, or anything else. Onward to the next Inktober, my friends!

ABOUT THE ILLUSTRATOR

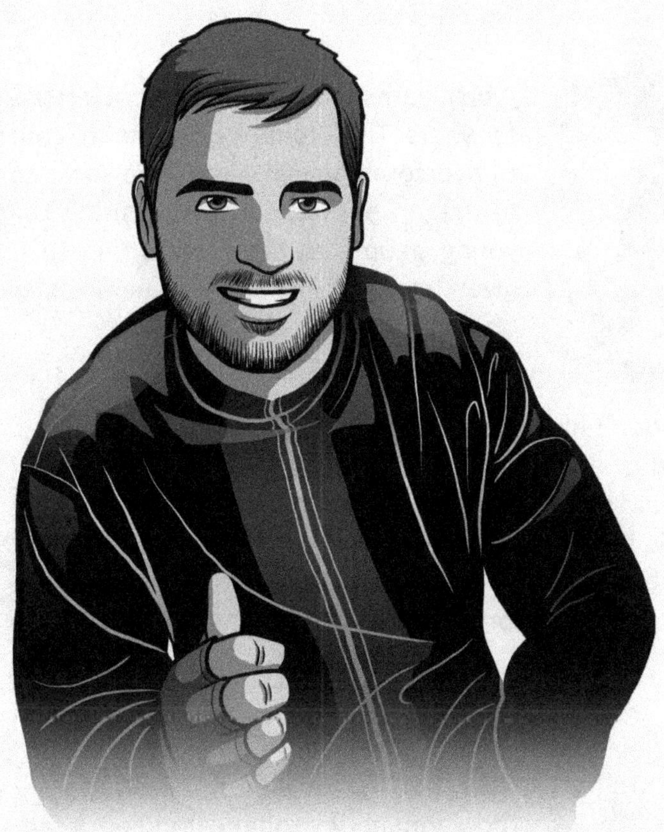

James Arthur Ville (1988 - present) was born in Guadalajara, Mexico but grew up in the United States of America. His passion for illustrating began at the age of 4. Watching television shows such as the Teenage Mutant Ninja Turtles and Dragon Ball Z inspired him to transition from pencil drawings to illustrating digitally. He spends most of his focus drawing for young audiences. From front covers to book illustrations, he's blessed to work from home where he can be close to his four children in Southern Oregon.

His most recent book is the Raising Dragons Graphic Novel, a comic book adaptation of the best-selling novel by Fantasy author, Bryan Davis. He looks forward to illustrating more graphic novels, either adaptations or his own stories. His favorite comic book artists include Scott McCloud, Art Spiegelman, Ken Akamatsu, and Akira Himekawa.

In his spare time, James enjoys playing video games with his kids. They also spend their weekends hiking and reading books. Visit jamesartville.com to see his latest illustrations and comics.

MORE FROM
JAMES ART VILLE

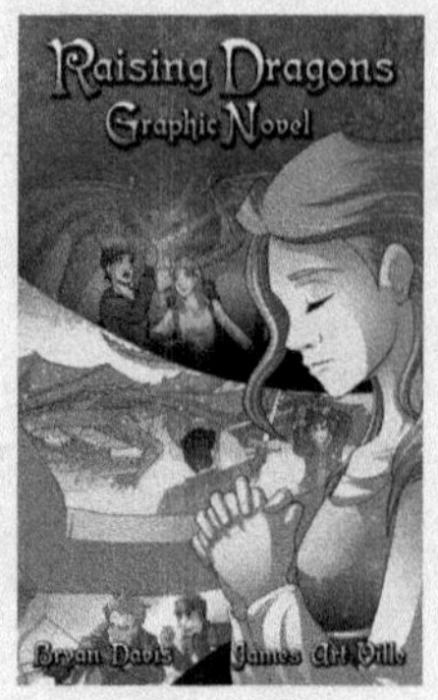

A boy learns of his dragon past; a girl has know of hers for years. They combine their faith, courage, and love to overcome an evil slayer who seeks to bring an end to dragon heritage, forever. Raising Dragons inspires young people to dig deep within to find their God given strengths and use them to overcome any obstacle.

Children don't have to be afraid of going to bed, even if the bed is out to get you! Young Walter Foley finds out the hard way just what it means to battle with bed time. This humorous tale is appropriate for children of all ages. Bryan Davis crafts a wonderful tale in rhyme and the color illustrations bring the story to life.

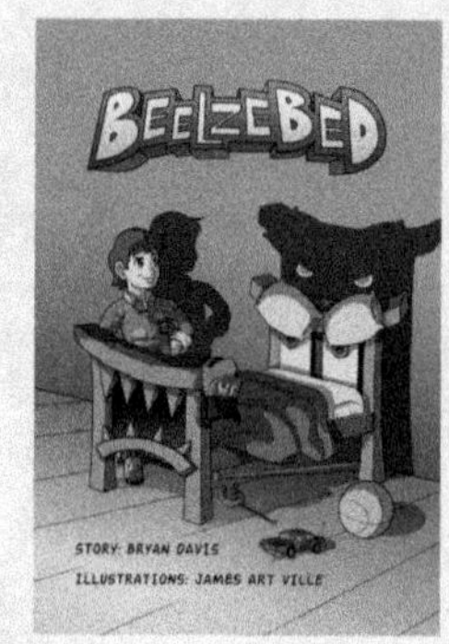

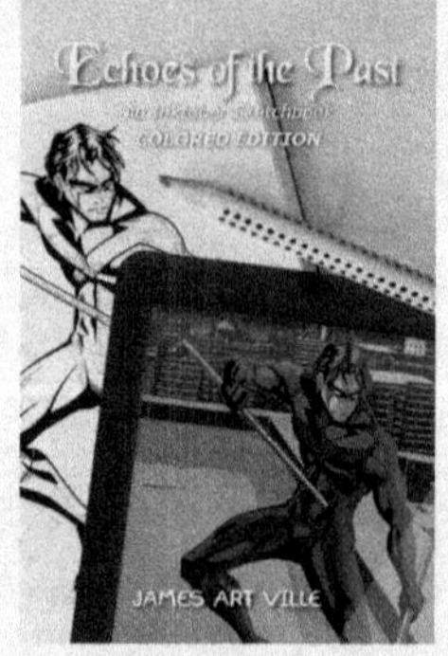

Collection of colored illustrations as part of the annual Inktober tradition. James Art Ville accepted the challenge of drawing every day during the month of October in 2017. Instead of adhering to the official calendar, he took inspiration from the artwork of his childhood featuring his favorite characters. Seeing the progression is inspiring!

Sketch Art Ville - The First Draft is a collection of pencil drawings from as early as 2008. For more than a decade he has doodled, drafted, sketched, and inked many characters and creatures. This includes original content, commissioned work, and fan art. There is a story of growth, discovery, and passion told through years worth of drawings.

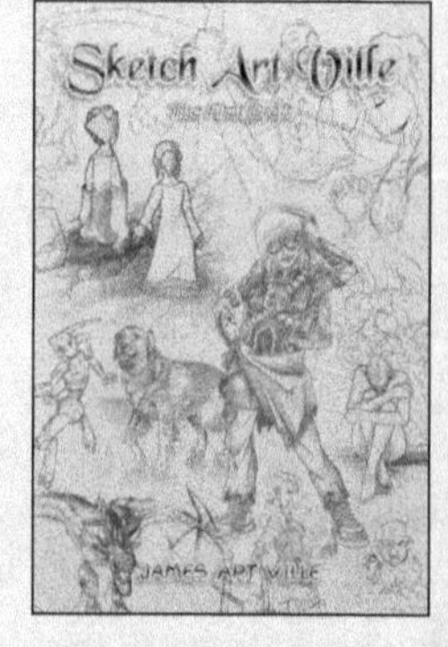

9 781951 907044